THE GHOST WRITER

THE GHOST WRITER

By Andrew Lawrenson

Published by Pyrian Publishing

The Ghost Writer

ISBN 978-1-910980-12-5 (Kindle)
ISBN 978-1-910980-13-2 (Paperback)
ISBN 978-1-910980-14-9 (Hardback)

Published by Pyrian Publishing
info@pyrian.co.uk

2 4 6 8 10 9 7 5 3 1

For Karen

"Now I know what a ghost is. Unfinished business, that's what."

— Salman Rushdie, The Satanic Verses

"Until you understand who I am, I will never be free."

— Ed Steele, The Haunting of Lady Jane

Prologue.

I used to think that death was the end; the final chapter of your life, a brief postscript to your existence, and then... nothing.

It's easy now to see where that all changed. Easy to divide it into before and after. Before I knew what terrors could lurk in the darkness that surrounds us all.

My life had already taken its own dark turn – a failed marriage and messy divorce following several unhappy years with my wife – but I wasn't yet aware of just how much darker it would become, nor of the light that lay on the other side.

Most people who hear my story find it hard to believe. Most just believe it to be the whimsical imagination of a desperate writer, but that doesn't bother me. Deep down inside I know it to be true, and in the end isn't that what really matters?

Let me tell you a story about the time when my whole life changed...

Chapter 1.

I was brought out of my slumber by a harsh buzzing noise from somewhere nearby. I reluctantly opened my eyes, trying to locate the source of the disturbance, but the room was dim and murky with only a thin sliver of pale grey light peeking in from under the door.

As I slowly came back to consciousness, I finally recognized the cause of the buzzing: my phone, on silent but still vibrating furiously, rattling its way across a hard surface.

I sat up, and then wished I hadn't. My head was throbbing with a dull headache, an unwelcome reminder of how much I had drunk the previous night.

Lifting up the cardboard box containing the leftovers of last night's pizza, I found my phone, gliding its way across the table. Glancing at its screen, I could see that it was Steve, my agent.

'Hi, Steve,' I groaned, putting the call onto speakerphone. The pain in my head was pounding, my mouth dry. A quick glance at the time on my phone told me that it was almost noon.

'How's my favourite client?' crackled Steve's cheerful voice out of the loudspeaker.

'Doing just fine,' I lied. I traipsed over to the window and pulled back the thick curtains slightly, wincing at the sunlight that flooded in. Outside was the uninspiring view of the hotel's car park.

'You're still on target for the start of summer? We're going to need it by then to have a chance of getting it out before Christmas.'

I was the author of a string of novels starring a husband and wife team who solved murder mysteries. Nothing that was going to win any awards, nothing to trouble the New York Times best seller lists, but enough to provide a living. Barely.

'Yeah, should be fine,' I lied again. 'I'm just having trouble with a couple of sections. I need to work it through in my mind.' In truth, I'd barely written anything since my divorce had been finalized six weeks ago. I wasn't just having trouble coming up with new ideas, this was full-blown writer's block. My heart wasn't in it anymore, and whenever I tried to sit down and write, my mind would either go blank or start to fixate on my wife. My *ex*-wife, I reminded myself. It wasn't as if I could just stop either. I was barely making enough from my books to make a living before the divorce, and now I had maintenance and child care payments to take into account as well. I knew that if I didn't get a new book out before Christmas it would put a serious dent in my sales and from there my bank account.

'I thought I'd give you a ring to see if you were still looking for a place to live?' said Steve, bringing me out of my daze.

I looked around at the cheap hotel room that had been my home for the last few weeks. The carpet was grubby, the wallpaper faded and peeling. Most of the surfaces were covered in dirty clothes or rubbish.

'Yeah, I'm still looking,' I groaned.

'As it happens,' said Steve, 'I've just heard about a new place that's become available.'

'I didn't know you were also an estate agent on the side?'

Steve gave a little chuckle. 'I heard about this place through work. This is *business*...it has literary connections.'

'What do you mean?' I asked, shaking my head in confusion, even though Steve couldn't see me.

'Do you remember Ed Steele?'

I thought for a moment. 'That horror writer from the eighties? Author of *The Dawn of the Devil* and *Journey from Hell*?'

'That's the one.'

'Well, what about him?'

'According to a good friend of mine, an old house of his is now available to rent. He hasn't lived there for years and rather than just continue to pump money into maintenance for no good reason, he decided to sell up. It was bought by a high-end letting company.'

'Where is it?' I asked, as I lumbered towards the bathroom to grab a glass of water.

'Deepest, darkest Devon. It's a cottage on the edge of a rural village, miles away from any distractions. Should be the perfect place to get some peace and quiet, allow you to concentrate and finish off your book.'

Allow me to start *my book*, I thought quietly to myself.

'Maybe it'll inspire you the same way it inspired him?' continued Steve enthusiastically.

'What do you mean?'

'This house is where he wrote all his famous novels, including *The Ghost's Tale*, the novel that kicked it all off for him. Only his last book was written somewhere else.'

'And you reckon I could do the same?'

'It couldn't hurt, could it?' Even though I couldn't see him, I could still imagine the grin on Steve's face as he said this. He was always painfully optimistic.

'Devon's not exactly next door. And I still have to look after Lisa at the weekends.' My wife had main custody of our daughter after the divorce, but at least I got to see her at regular intervals.

'It's not as far as you think, and the motorway will take you most of the way there. It's got three bedrooms and it comes fully furnished, so there should be no problem having Lisa there with you.'

I had to admit, sharing a house would be a lot more convenient than adjoining hotel rooms.

'The minimum lease is three months, so you don't have to commit too much,' he added.

'Are you on commission or something?' I chuckled.

'Just thinking of my favourite client,' said Steve. 'I knew you were looking, so when my friend mentioned it to me, I immediately thought of you.'

'I don't know...' I said. 'I've always been a bit of a townie.'

'Well then, maybe this is the change you need. Make a break of things, get a change of scenery and force some inspiration into you.'

'The divorce *has* been putting a bit of a shadow over everything,' I agreed. 'Maybe I could do with getting away from it all – an extended holiday if nothing else.'

'Well, I wouldn't let the taxman hear you say that. I reckon you could probably cover it as a business expense if your accountant is creative enough.'

I looked once more at the mess all around me and sighed again. 'Okay. Can you look into it for me? Don't commit to anything just yet – just check it's still available, what the cost is going to be, that kind of thing?'

'Sure, will do. But if it's still available, you may need to move quickly, so start having a serious think about it. I'll email you the details.'

Chapter 2

My agent had said the house was rural, but I hadn't figured on just how remote it would be. I had been driving for ninety minutes, and it had been almost half an hour since I had left the wide fast lanes of the motorway behind. Now I was driving my car cautiously down narrow country lane after narrow country lane as they twisted and turned through the Devon landscape, slavishly following directions from my phone's GPS.

Just when I thought I had reached the dead centre of nowhere, it suddenly announced that I had arrived at my destination. I slowed the car to a gradual halt, wondering where on earth the house was meant to be. At first all I could see was a thick forest of trees to my left and a high countryside hedge to my right, but then I spotted something. Twenty yards down the road, masked by the tall trees of the forest, was a dirt road. From where I sat I could just make out a small wooden plaque nailed to one of the trunks, so I put the car back in gear and crept closer to read what it said. As I drew near I could see the name *Lake View Cottage* printed on it in a neat but faded script.

This was the place. I switched on my indicator, despite not having seen another car for minutes, and then turned slowly into the narrow lane. It was little more than a dirt path, two rough earthen tracks with a ridge of grass down the middle. I followed it carefully as it lazily wound its way through the dense woods, repeatedly slowing the car down to a crawl as I navigated holes and ruts in the ground. Whenever I veered too close to either side of the path, smaller branches from the trees and bushes lining either side would scrape agonizingly against the side of my car. After patiently following the road as it zigged and zagged around some of the larger trees, I finally emerged, squinting into the setting sun that now lay before me.

Lake View Cottage sat directly in front of me. The building itself was a compact Georgian cottage built from grey bricks, two storeys tall with small dormer windows in the roof. I approached slowly and could see the large eponymous lake not far from the rear of the house. It was blue-grey in colour, perfectly flat and still, stretching off into the distance between two low hills.

As I drew away from the forest and neared the house, the path gradually turned from dirt and rock into a gravel driveway, and I drew the car to a halt just outside the front door. Turning off the engine and climbing out, I had my first real look around the area.

The view was spectacular. To the front of the house were the woods I had driven through, and to the rear was the lake. Either side, beyond the spacious gardens, were farmers' fields as far as the eye could see, a flock of sheep grazing half a mile away up the hill. Trees and bushes littered the gardens around the house, with almost an orchard of apple trees on one side.

It was peaceful too, with only the distant sounds of birds for company. For a man who had spent his entire life living in towns and cities, it was almost eerily quiet; it felt almost too quiet, as if someone had turned down the volume of life. The only movement was the swaying of branches in the wind as it carried the distant bird song. A shiver came over me as I stood there looking over the lake, feeling almost as if someone was watching me, although I knew that couldn't be true; the nearest neighbour was almost a quarter of a mile away, up around the other side of the forest according to the maps I had looked at.

I contemplated walking around the property and exploring the gardens, but as the icy wind blew around me, I decided that could wait. Instead, I pulled the key from the letting agency from my pocket, walking over to the solid wooden front door and slipping it into the lock. It turned easily with a sturdy click, and I grasped the old brass handle, the door swinging inwards without so much as a squeak.

The hallway was small but well lit, with the muted rays of the setting sun coming in through a large sash window at the top of the stairs. Two wooden doors stood closed on either side of me, a final glass-panelled door at the end of the hall.

I took a look in the door to my left first: a living room fitted out in a modern style, complete with leather sofa and large flat-screen TV. The door to my right led into the dining room, which ran along the side of the house and opened up into the kitchen at the rear. The dining room was bright and airy, a stream of daylight flooding in through the large French doors and bathing the room with a dark golden hue.

I stepped to the doors and looked out over the gardens, squinting slightly in the light. Immediately on the other side was a spacious patio with wooden furniture and barbeque, as well as a well, which I had been informed was fully functional – the whole house was supplied with water from the same source that fed the lake. Beyond the patio was a long garden, which ended with steps down to a path that led to the lake beyond. A small jetty extended out into the water, but it looked like access to it was blocked by a short wooden fence.

Beyond the dining room was the kitchen and utility room at the rear of the house, complete with all the amenities you would hope for: a washing machine, tumble drier and dishwasher. On the kitchen table was a bowl of flowers from the letting company, as well as a folder full of documents and information about the house.

Upstairs there were three bedrooms, two single and one master, as well as a master bathroom with a huge antique iron bathtub. The first-floor landing ended in a steep narrow staircase up to a small attic door, but when I tried it, the handle wouldn't turn; it was locked. I shrugged and headed back downstairs again, taking my bags from the car and dumping them in the hallway for now.

It had been a long day and I was already tired, so I decided to have a bite to eat before I finished unpacking. I would have to try and find some shops in the morning to stock up with food, but for now I had brought enough for a light snack. I made myself a quick sandwich and then sat down in the dining room, looking out at the sun setting over the lake as I ate.

The house was pleasant enough, but there was still something about it that left me feeling unsettled. I had never been a great traveller, and maybe this house was just a bit too remote. I was all alone out here, probably further from any other living soul than at any point in my life. To someone like me, it felt unnaturally quiet and isolated. I had to admit though, the view of the lake was spectacular.

I stood up again, heading back to the living room to turn the television on. I didn't care what was on; I just needed some background noise, some link back to civilization, no matter how distant. I lay down on the sofa and closed my eyes, breathing slowly and gradually sinking into the cushions.

I knew that I should be writing, or at least I ought to be *trying* to write. But I was just too tired. I couldn't think straight. It could wait until the morning; a fresh start to a new life.

Chapter 3

The next morning I set about unpacking the rest of my belongings. Having thoroughly inspected all the rooms, I decided to use the oak dining room table as my writing desk and sat my laptop on it. From there I would have a great view of the lake and surrounding countryside. Thankfully, the letting company had installed a wi-fi internet connection here; the speed wasn't great, not what I was used to from living in a city centre, but I would have to make do.

After making myself a strong cup of coffee, I sat down at the table, ready to try writing again. I had a change of scenery, a new environment to try and stimulate my senses – but try as I might, I just couldn't make the words come.

I stared at the few pages I had written previously. I had written them not long before the divorce; they were just placeholders really, with no real plot or narrative. I stared at the words again and again for over an hour, but just couldn't think of where to go next.

The plot of the book had hardly even been started, and I still had no real idea where I was going to go with the story. I supposed that if I was going to get something out in time for Christmas I would have to stick with safe formulas that I knew my audience would like. Dig out a few clichés. Rehash a few well-worn plots. But even that wouldn't come to me. The change of scenery hadn't been the miracle cure that I'd been hoping for, at least not yet.

Lunchtime came and went, and still I was no further along, growing more and more frustrated with my lack of progress. I needed to do something, *anything*. I pushed the laptop away from me in disgust and stood up. Perhaps a walk; get some fresh air and see if the actual countryside could inspire me, rather than just a view of it through a window. I put on my walking boots and a coat, letting myself out through the back door and into the rear gardens.

There was an overgrown path at the back of the house, winding through the middle of a small grove of apple trees with steps leading down to a gravel path that followed the lake's edge. I set off down it, the small stones crunching noisily under my feet. As I neared the water's edge, I could see the small wooden jetty more clearly, and could see it wasn't in a good state. The old wooden boards looked in danger of rotting away completely. A metal gate at the near end stood padlocked, the padlock distinctly newer than anything else around – probably put there by the letting company to stop anyone having a nasty accident. I decided to ignore it, continuing on along the path, which took me around the side of the wood and up the incline of the hill. As I turned around a bend at the edge of the forest, an old stone farmhouse came into view. A middle-aged woman was standing on the patio at the rear of the building, hanging washing out on a line. I gave her a friendly wave as I passed, and she waved back with a polite smile.

Leaving the house behind, I carried on up the hill and passed farmers' fields populated with sheep and cows. Then, as I topped the crest, I could finally see the small village of Treleven before me, not much more than a small church and a couple of local shops, sat in the middle of the few dozen houses.

I wandered down the other side of the hill in the warm sunshine, the going easier now that I wasn't working against gravity. The footpath wound its way past more fields before eventually leading me to the rear of the village church, its dry stone walls loose and crumbling around the edges. There was no obvious way around, so I took the direct path through the graveyard, which occupied the bulk of the church grounds. A door was open at the rear of the chapel through which I could see a man I took to be the local vicar. He gave me a polite wave as I passed and I returned the wave with a smile, carrying on and emerging through the front gates where a small sign declared this church to be *St Mary's*.

The road I found myself on was quiet and peaceful with no traffic, just an old man in the distance walking his dog. I strolled along now at a casual pace, down the slight incline and towards the small village shop I could see up on the corner – while I was here I might as well stock up on some provisions. I could see a stack of papers sitting by the door, two tables of fruit and vegetables planted in front of the shop's windows.

As I pushed open the door and stepped inside, there was a little tinkle from a small bell above the door to announce my entrance. Behind the counter stood a man who looked at least sixty, with short grey hair and a thin wiry frame. He looked up from his newspaper, peering over the top of his glasses as he heard me enter.

'Can I help you?' he asked with a friendly smile. He had a pleasant West Country accent.

'Just browsing,' I replied almost instinctively. I was used to pushy salesmen in busy shops, but from the look of this man, he was anything but. From what I'd seen of the village so far, this shop probably didn't get much trade from people just passing through; I may have been the first new face he'd seen in here in weeks. 'I've just moved into the old Lake View Cottage,' I added. 'You know the place?'

This seemed to catch the old man's attention, and he nodded slowly. 'That didn't take too long,' he said with an air of surprise. 'Many round here were surprised when the letting company bought that old place. It's been vacant for decades. Didn't think many would want to rent a house round these parts.'

'Why not, if you don't mind me asking?'

'We're just very out of the way here in our village. Not really an easy commute to anywhere. Not close enough to the sea to be a traditional retirement village or holiday destination. Most of the folks here have lived in the village all their lives.'

'I see,' I said.

'So what made you want to come and join our little community then?'

I shrugged. 'I actually *wanted* somewhere out of the way... somewhere where I could concentrate without too many distractions. I'm an author,' I added by way of explanation.

'Anything I'd heard of?'

'I'm Peter Banner,' I said. 'I've got a series of detective novels.'

The shopkeeper gave a little shrug and shook his head. 'Sorry.' Then he added, 'I'm not much of reader, though. That's more of my wife's thing.'

I couldn't think of anything to add, so I picked up a beaten old wire basket from the floor next to the counter and proceeded to pick out a few basic items. The shopkeeper went back to reading his newspaper.

I wandered up and down the short aisles, adding a few things to my basket: some bread, milk, sausages, some tins of soup, a newspaper. When I was finished, I placed it on the counter and the shopkeeper proceeded to ring it through the till, putting the items into thin plastic bags for me.

As I fetched my wallet from my pocket, I glanced at the shelves on the wall behind the counter where several bottles of spirits were kept on display. 'Do you have any decent whisky?' I asked.

The shopkeeper paused in his packing and looked up at me. 'Some reasonable stuff,' he said, 'but nothing too fancy.' He picked up a bottle from the shelf, peering down his nose at the label and then holding it out to me so that I could see for myself. 'This one here's a quite nice ten-year-old single malt Scotch.' From the price label that was attached to the bottle, it ought to be.

I gave him a nod and he added it to the shopping. I could still afford it, at least for now, and it didn't look like there would be much else to do around here.

The shopkeeper put the whisky into a separate bag for me as I handed over a fistful of notes, receiving a pitiful amount of change back again.

'So what do folks do around here?' I asked.

'Do?'

'For entertainment?'

He gave a little laugh. 'If you're after any big-city thrills, then you're best off driving into Exeter or Torquay, although they still might not have what you want. Folks here pretty much keep to themselves. There's the church, of course. They have several evening services and a couple of coffee mornings, but you don't strike me as the church-going type.'

I shrugged. He had me there.

'There's the village pub, *The Eight Bells*,' he said as he handed me the bag with the bottle of whisky in it. 'That strikes me as possibly more your kind of thing.'

I took the bag from him, before following it with the others from the counter. 'And that's it?'

'We're a simple lot, us country folk.'

I couldn't tell if he was being serious or taking the piss. I decided not to push the point.

'Well, many thanks,' I said. 'I'm sure I'll see you again soon.'

After a simple dinner of sausages and mashed potatoes, I pushed my plate away, swapping it instead for my laptop. I turned it on, and then as I waited for it to start up I decided that I would need something else first, before I tried to write. I went back to the kitchen and went through the cupboards until I found a nice crystal tumbler. The bottle of Scotch was still sitting on the kitchen counter from where I had unpacked it earlier, and I cracked it open, pouring a large measure into the glass.

I cursed momentarily, realizing that I had forgotten to buy any decent mineral water to go with it, but then remembered what the letting company had told me; the house was fed its water from the same underground source that filled the lake. There was even a well in the back garden if I was feeling adventurous. I added a few drops of water from the tap and then hesitantly took a small sip. The shopkeeper hadn't been lying – it was good.

Suitable armed, I wandered back to the dining room, turning off the main light. The room descended into shadows, the beckoning glare of the monitor now the sole focus of my attention. I slumped into the chair, bathed in the screen's phosphorescent glow, and returned to my barely started novel, still not quite sure what I was going to write. For twenty minutes I just stared at the screen, unable to even think of where to begin. In desperation, I forced myself simply to write anything – surely the problem was just starting, I told myself, and once I'd started I'd then find it easier to continue.

I managed to write a few lines, and slowly continued until I had managed a few paragraphs. I stopped and read back through what I had written. It was trash, and barely literate trash at that. I deleted it all without any hesitation.

I felt like the more I tried to force myself to write, the harder it was for the words to come, and the increasingly large glasses of whisky didn't seem to be helping. It hadn't always been this way; in happier times the words had seemed to flow from my subconscious onto the page almost on their own. I was starting to get desperate.

I glanced at my watch; it was getting late. The sun had gone down hours ago, and the moon had disappeared behind dark clouds so that I could no longer see the garden and grounds beyond the window; all I could see now was my own reflection. As I sat staring into space, rain began to fall from the sky, gently at first and then growing heavy, the wind blowing strongly across the open fields and making the raindrops pitter-patter on the glass. Still I persevered, struggling on with the novel, but just not able to find the words I wanted.

Maybe this is it, I thought to myself. Maybe there was only so much creativity in me, and now I'd used it all up. Maybe my wife had been my muse, and now that she had gone, so had my talent, so had my career...my life. For so many years, I had defined myself by my work, and now that was gone. I had sacrificed my marriage and family for my career, and now I had neither. Maybe it was time for a change.

I pushed the laptop away from me in disgust, out towards the centre of the table, and leant forwards, folding my arms and resting my head on them. I needed to clear my mind. I closed my eyes, breathing deeply. I desperately needed inspiration.

I jerked awake suddenly as I realized that I had nodded off. It was still dark outside, a storm now raging, although there was a glimmer of moonlight cast across the garden. I lifted up my arm and looked at my watch to see that it was almost one in the morning. Pushing my chair back, I stood up, only to have to sit straight back down again, the room spinning around me. *Damn*, I thought. I must have drunk more than I had thought.

I stood up again, taking it slowly and carefully this time, and turned to face the stairs; it was time to go to bed and worry about my book in the morning.

I staggered slowly out of the dining room, turning the light off as I went. As I took a few more steps towards the base of the stairs, I stopped. Out of the corner of my eye, I had glimpsed something. I could have sworn that I had seen something up above me – some movement in the pale moonlight that was coming in through the sash window on the landing. Was there somebody up there, hiding in the long shadows?

'Who's there?' I called into the darkness. I waited, but there was no reply, only the silence of the night and distant sounds of the storm.

'Hello?' I called again, taking a step forwards. Again there was no reply.

I stepped cautiously to the bottom of the stairs, flicking the light switch to illuminate the landing upstairs, blinking at the sudden brightness. As my vision cleared, I could only see an empty space. Slowly, I advanced up the stairs one by one.

'Is there anyone there?' I called as I reached the top, but I was starting to feel silly now. One by one, I went to each of the rooms, opening the door and looking inside, turning the light on in each. All of the rooms were empty; only the locked attic door defeated me.

A moment ago I would have sworn that there had been someone there, someone in the darkness of the landing looking down at me as I stood in the hallway, but with all the rooms checked, I was forced to conclude that it had just been my imagination – the product of too little sleep and too much whisky, as well as the house and its shadows being unfamiliar. I staggered into the bathroom and gave my teeth a half-hearted brush and got half-undressed, crashing onto my double bed and falling asleep almost immediately.

That night was the first in which I had the dream.

I was standing on the patio behind Lake View Cottage, looking up at the building as it stood before me, the low morning sunlight reflecting off the windows and making me squint. The lake lay behind me, and a cold wind was blowing over it, making me shiver despite the bright sunlight that didn't quite feel as warm as it should. There was the aroma of flowers and freshly cut grass in the air, and I could hear bird song in the distance that was unfamiliar but still strangely reassuring. I slowly approached the house, walking up to the bay doors, pulling them open and stepping inside. Something was different with the room, but I couldn't put my finger on exactly what it was. The layout and decor of the room had an odd feeling of being both old-fashioned and contemporary at the same time. I knew something was wrong, something was different, but I just couldn't put my finger on exactly what it was.

I turned to look at the dining room table and saw my laptop resting on it, just where I had left it. No, I suddenly realized – it wasn't my laptop, it was an old-fashioned typewriter. A sheet of paper was sticking up from it, a large pile of sheets lying on the table next to it. Now that I looked again, I couldn't understand how I could ever have mistaken it for a laptop.

From somewhere in the distance, I could hear the sound of running water, and I turned around, trying to locate the source. Something about that sound made me feel nervous, although I couldn't articulate exactly why. It was a perfectly normal, innocent noise but there was something about it that struck fear into my soul.

I was starting to feel uneasy in the pit of my stomach, as if aware of a great danger approaching. With great trepidation, I took a step towards the hallway, heading for the source of the noise. First one step and then another, moving in slow motion as if I was wading through deep water.

I awoke with a jump to the sound of the alarm clock beeping next to my bed. My heart was racing, my hands shaking, a pounding ache in my head. I felt as if I'd hardly slept at all. I swore that I would have to lay off the whisky before going to bed.

Chapter 4

I sat up in my bed, stretching my arms and yawning hard. There was sunlight streaming in through the bedroom windows; I hadn't even managed to close the curtains the previous night. The light was altogether too bright and my head was throbbing with a monster of a hangover.

My dream – I was hesitant to call it a nightmare – was fading rapidly from my memory. What little I could recall had rattled me though, and I took a few moments to regain my composure before swinging my legs out of bed.

I stood up on unsteady legs, taking off the rest of my clothes from the previous night and staggering over to the bathroom where I brushed my teeth and took a shower. When that was done I shaved, and at that point felt almost human apart from the thumping headache. I slipped into some fresh clothes and plodded downstairs to the kitchen where I found some paracetamol in a cupboard above the oven. I took a couple with a glass of water while I made myself a strong coffee.

I was thinking about making myself some lunch – something light, maybe some soup, maybe a sandwich – when there was a knock at the door.

This took me by surprise. I wasn't expecting anyone, and the house seemed a bit out of the way to attract people calling door to door. Had I arranged for anything to be delivered? I didn't think so.

With a scratch of my head, I put down my coffee and wandered over to the front door. Pulling it open, I was greeted by the sight a woman standing on my doorstep, an old silver Volkswagen Golf on the driveway behind her. For a second I struggled to place her until it suddenly came to me – she was the woman I had seen in the nearby farmhouse hanging up the washing.

She appeared to be in her mid-thirties, and I now realized that what I had previously taken to be greying hair was actually ash blonde; it hung straight down to her shoulders, nicely framing her thin face with high cheek bones. Her deep blue eyes seemed to sparkle as she smiled at me, almost hypnotically. I was standing there studying her face, when it occurred to me that she had been standing there for several seconds and I had yet to say anything.

'I'm sorry,' I spluttered awkwardly. 'You took me by surprise – I wasn't expecting anyone. Can I help you?'

'Actually, I'm here to see if I can help you,' she said with a polite smile. She held up her arms and I saw that she was holding a small bouquet of flowers and a bottle of wine. 'I live next door... Well, I'm your nearest neighbour anyway. I didn't know who you were when you passed by the other day, but then I heard that someone had moved into this old property and I put two and two together. I thought I'd come round and welcome you to the neighbourhood.'

'It doesn't take long for news to spread round here then.'

She shrugged and smiled. 'It's a small village. There's not much that happens here, and news of what little does happen tends to spread like wildfire.'

It suddenly struck me that I wasn't being a very cordial host. It had been a while since I'd had any women standing on my doorstep offering me wine and flowers.

'I'm sorry,' I said sheepishly, standing back and opening the door wider. 'Where are my manners? Please come in.'

She gave a cheerful smile and stepped inside, graciously offering the wine and flowers, which I took from her.

'You needn't have worried yourself about these,' I said, and then realized that this might have come across as sounding a bit dismissive. 'But they're very nice,' I added, trying to compensate.

'It's no worry, really,' she said. 'It's not often you get a new neighbour around here.'

'I'll just find something to put these in.' She followed me into the kitchen, where I started opening all the cupboards looking for something to put the flowers in. Eventually I found a tall jug branded with a *Pimms* logo. It would have to do for now.

'Sorry,' I muttered. 'I've only just moved in, and I'm still not sure where everything is.'

She nodded a graceful acknowledgement.

I filled the jug with water from the sink and then put the flowers into it, finally placing them onto the windowsill.

'I'm sorry,' I said almost automatically, and then wanted to kick myself. I'd barely done anything but apologize since I'd opened the door to her. I took a deep breath to momentarily compose myself. 'I still haven't introduced myself. I'm Peter – Peter Banner.'

'I'm Madeline,' she said, extending a graceful hand, 'but everyone calls me Maddy.' I took her hand and we shook. Her handshake was firm but delicate.

'Would you like a cup of coffee?' I asked as our hands separated. 'Or tea? I think we have some tea.'

'Coffee would be fine – black, no sugar.'

'Okay, I can definitely manage that,' I said as I filled the kettle and turned it on.

Maddy leaned back against the kitchen counter, taking an approving glance up and down the kitchen. 'So what brings you to our little village?' she asked. 'Business or pleasure? If that's not too personal a question...'

'No, not at all,' I said.

'People always tell me I'm too nosy,' she said with a grin and a glint in her eye. 'But I guess that's what comes of living alone in a small village.'

'It's actually a bit of both,' I said. 'I'm a writer, and thought a change of scene might do me some good. Inspire me, if you know what I mean?'

Maddy nodded and grinned back at me. 'That's quite a coincidence – you'll never guess who used to live here...'

I gave a little chuckle. 'Not a coincidence at all. In fact, that's why my agent recommended I come here – I think he hopes a bit of Ed Steele's inspiration might rub off on me. I could certainly do with his share of book sales.'

Just as I finished speaking, the kettle turned itself off as it finished boiling. I grabbed a pot of instant coffee from the cupboard, spooning some into a couple of mugs.

'I've only got instant,' I apologized. 'My wife's got the coffee machine.'

Maddy gave a casual wave of her hand to indicate this was fine. 'So you're married then?'

'Divorced,' I sighed. 'I suppose I really ought to call her my ex-wife, although that still sounds strange to me. I suppose it won't after a time.'

'So have you written anything I might have read?' asked Maddy, diverting the topic of conversation back to my profession. 'Peter Banner,' she muttered to herself. 'I'm afraid the name doesn't really ring any bells, although I have to confess that I don't read too many books – and when I do, it's mainly period dramas.'

'*The Courageous Corpse... The Masonic Murders*?' I asked. Those had been my two biggest sellers. 'I mainly write thrillers,' I added. 'Gabriel Keys and his wife, Harriet, who solve mysteries together?' For a brief moment I wondered about divorcing my two protagonists, splitting up their happy marriage. That would be something I could relate to, and just maybe it might help me start writing again... but it wouldn't go down at all well with my fans. It would probably just kill off the entire series of books – not that I could see a prosperous future for them at the moment anyway. Better to go out with a bang than just fade away, I supposed.

'Sorry,' she said, bringing me back to the moment. She gave a polite grimace and a shrug. 'Doesn't ring a bell.'

'That's okay,' I said with a shake of my head. 'You're in the majority, much to my agent's annoyance.'

'Well, I'll be sure to keep an eye open for your books next time I'm at the library.'

'What about you, Maddy?' I asked. 'What do you do for a living?'

'Not too much now. I'm widowed...'

'I'm sorry,' I interjected, but she waved it away with another swipe of her hand.

'It was a long time ago now,' she said. 'But these days I work part-time over at the local council – in the welfare department.'

'That sounds...' I paused for a moment, trying to think of what to say. '...Interesting,' was all I could manage.

She gave a short mirthless laugh. 'It's really not. The job description makes it sound like you'd be spending all your time helping people, but it's really just tons of paperwork. Or whatever the equivalent is, now that it's all on computers.'

'And what about when you're not working?'

She sighed slightly. I think it was the first time I hadn't seen her with a smile on her face. 'Not too much. I do a lot of walking, help out in a charity shop the next village over, do some painting.'

'Painting? What kind of thing?'

'Landscapes mainly. Just watercolours. Nothing fancy; it just keeps me amused.'

'Do you sell any?'

'Goodness, no,' she said with an embarrassed shudder. 'I've got an attic full of them.'

'You should put on a show somewhere,' I suggested. 'Display them in a gallery.'

She gave an embarrassed grimace and shrugged. 'They're really not that good.'

'You haven't seen some of the exhibitions I've been to at small galleries. As long as they're recognizable as landscapes, I'm sure you'd be fine.'

She replied with a polite smile but didn't say anything. I wondered if I'd hit a nerve and decided to change the subject. 'You must get awfully lonely out here on your own. You've never thought about moving somewhere...well, somewhere a bit less isolated?'

'I've lived here all my life,' she said. 'My parents owned my house before me, until they died just over a decade ago. I couldn't imagine living anywhere else.'

She took another sip of her coffee and glanced at her watch as she said this. 'Look at the time,' she said, 'I'm afraid I really ought to get going – I have to be at work in half an hour.'

'Well thanks again for the wine and flowers,' I said. 'You really didn't need to, but they're very gratefully received.'

That evening after dinner, I sat down at the living room table and powered up my laptop.

Once again, I was finding it impossible to write, but something was different this time. It was no longer my ex-wife that preyed on my mind, haunting and distracting me. Now it was Maddy that I kept returning to, the image of her smiling face in my mind. My inability to write no longer seemed to be as much of an issue.

Chapter 5

Today was a Saturday, and while my ex had custody of our daughter during the week, at the weekends it was normally my chance to spend some time with her. I pulled myself briskly from my bed at just past seven, when the sun was only just rising over the horizon and the air was still crisp and cold – I had forgotten to adjust the central heating to come on earlier today.

I managed to grab a quick bowl of cereal and a cup of coffee before clambering into my car and heading off towards the motorway and from there to my old house. As I drove, I mentally chastised myself for still thinking of it as my old house rather than what it actually was now: my ex-wife's house.

The drive back to the city was quiet, too early in the morning for much traffic to have built up at the weekend. As I drew near, I checked the time on the car's entertainment system. It was ten to nine, just a few minutes before I had arranged to pick up Lisa.

When I arrived in her street, I pulled up in a parking space in the street outside, but instead of going to the door I got out my phone instead, texting my daughter to tell her I was there. I told myself that it was still early for the weekend and I didn't want to wake anyone by ringing the doorbell, but I knew I wasn't fooling anyone, above all myself. I just didn't want to have to talk to my wife. My ex-wife, I corrected myself again. I especially didn't want to have to talk to her new boyfriend if he was there. That hadn't gone at all well last time.

Five minutes later, Lisa emerged, reluctantly kissing her mother good-bye. She waved goodbye to our daughter, but only gave a scant glance in my direction. Lisa jogged across the street, opening the boot to deposit a couple of bags inside before opening the passenger door and climbing in.

'Are you good to go?' I asked her.

'Yep.'

'Got everything? Pyjamas, toothbrush?'

'I'm not five anymore, dad. I can look after myself.'

'Okay,' I replied defensively. 'Just checking.' I indicated and then pulled out into the empty road, heading out of the city and back towards Dorset.

'How's your mum doing?' I asked as we rejoined the main roads and I settled into a steady cruise.

'She's doing okay. Her and Rupert seem to be quite happy together.'

I gave a small involuntary shiver as I heard the name and hoped that Lisa didn't notice.

'It's not his fault,' said Lisa, who obviously *had* noticed. 'She has a right to be happy too, and well, when you–'

'I know, I know,' I said, cutting her off. I really didn't want to hear about how well they were getting along.

'He's not going to replace you,' she said. 'You know it's you who'll always be my dad.'

'I know,' I replied, a small smile on my face. The conversation descended into silence for a few minutes until I spoke up again. 'Have you got any plans for the weekend? What do you want to do?'

'Not much. I've got a ton of homework and revision. I thought I'd mainly get on with that.'

'Well, you should have all the peace and quiet you need to help you concentrate.'

'Tell me you have broadband at your new place.'

'Yes,' I nodded. 'But the speed's not great. It won't be quite what you're used to.'

Lisa sighed noisily, taking her phone out of her handbag and turning it on. 'Tell me you've at least got 4G there?'

I shrugged. I hadn't actually checked, but I doubted it. It looked like this might be a long weekend.

✳   ✳   ✳

When we arrived back at Lake View Cottage, I took my daughter's bags out of the boot while she remained in the car, staring at a game on her phone and occasionally tapping the screen frenetically. Whatever she was playing, it had kept her captivated for the last half hour of the journey.

I had started heading to the house when I heard a call of 'Smile, dad!' and I turned to see what she wanted.

Lisa was standing by the car, holding her phone out; she was taking a picture of the pair of us in front of the house. I put the bags down and came over to stand next to her, a wide grin on my face. She took a couple of selfies, and when she was happy slid her phone back into her pocket. I picked up the bags again, carrying them across the threshold and then dropping them in the hall.

'I thought I'd put you in the blue room,' I said.

'The blue room?'

'Sorry. I just named the bedrooms after their colours. You're in the one with the blue wallpaper. Why don't you go check it out while I put the kettle on?'

She picked up the smaller of her two bags and started up the stairs, while I headed into the kitchen and put the kettle on, fetching the coffee and a couple of mugs. When she came back down, I had a steaming cup of coffee ready for her.

'Here you go,' I said, handing it to her.

'Thanks, dad,' she replied politely.

'Find your room okay?'

'Yeah. This place isn't *that* large.'

'I'm going to make some lunch in a minute. Sandwiches okay?'

She nodded by way of reply. 'I might go have a quick look around outside, if that's okay?'

'Knock yourself out. I'll be right here. Just wipe your shoes when you come back in. It's quite muddy out there.'

She walked over to the back door, unlocking it and stepping outside. The sky was clear and the sun was starting to come out from behind the clouds; it was turning into a nice day.

She returned fifteen minutes later, letting herself back in and taking off her muddy shoes.

'Find everything okay?' I asked.

'There's not a lot to find,' she replied. I couldn't help but hear a hint of disappointment in her voice. She pulled out her phone, glancing at the screen. 'Have you got the wi-fi password?' she asked. 'The reception here is awful. Barely any signal at all, let alone any data.'

'Lake View,' I told her. 'One word, all lowercase.'

She typed it into her phone. 'I don't suppose you need to worry about your neighbours stealing your wi-fi out here, do you. You don't *have* any neighbours.'

'Not any close enough to use our wi-fi...' I agreed.

The expression on her face seemed to pick up as her phone connected. She was back in contact with the world again. She picked up a plate from the table, on which I had put a sandwich and some fruit.

'Where are you going?' I asked.

'I thought I'd eat in my room while I do some work,' she replied as she shuffled out of the room staring at her phone screen. 'Bring up my other bag, will you?'

✳ ✳ ✳

While Lisa was upstairs hopefully working on her schoolwork, I took the opportunity to try and work some more on my novel. I seated myself at the dining room table and turned on the laptop, glancing out at the landscape through the windows while it started up. The sun had successfully managed to find its way out from behind the clouds for a little while, and the sunlight was reflecting off the smooth lake surface. I turned back to gaze at my laptop, the barrenness of the lake echoed in the empty page that lay before me.

I was still staring at a mostly empty page when I heard Lisa coming back down the stairs. A quick glance at the clock in the corner of my screen told me that I had been at this for almost two hours, with only a few lines of fairly terrible prose to show for it.

'You okay?' I asked without looking up from my laptop.

'Meh,' she replied simply.

'What is it?'

'My room's cold,' she said. 'And...'

'What?' I asked. 'What's the matter?'

'This place gives me the creeps.'

'The creeps? Why?'

'I don't know,' she shrugged casually. 'It's just so quiet and isolated. *Lonely*. The rest of the world could have disappeared and you wouldn't even know. Plus...I don't know. There's just something about this house. It gives me the chills.'

'Really? I'd have thought you'd be beyond all that at your age.' I stood up. 'I'm going to cook dinner in a bit. What do you want?'

'Can we eat out? I'd rather not stay here all evening?'

'There aren't a lot of restaurants nearby.'

'Yeah, but there must be loads of country pubs that serve food that we could drive to. *Please* dad...'

'Okay,' I sighed. Lisa had a sad pouty look on her face that I was always a sucker for. I looked at my watch. 'It's a bit early yet, though. Give me another hour to work and then we'll set off.'

It was half-past six when we arrived at *The Cricketers Arms*, a family-friendly pub a couple of villages over. From a quick look online, it had looked like the best choice, and as I opened the door into a warm friendly atmosphere I knew I had made a good decision. It was cold outside and they had a roaring open fire going in the fireplace. We pulled up a couple of chairs and sat down at a small table, soaking up the warmth and hospitality.

'Did I ever tell you about the person who lived in the house before me?' I asked as we were setting into our dinner – a steak for me, a burger for Lisa.

'No, I don't think so,' she replied, wiping some ketchup from the corner of her mouth.

'He was also an author.'

'Like you?'

I chuckled. 'A lot more successful than me. He had a string of bestseller novels in the eighties. Pretty much one a year for the entire decade.'

'What type of books?'

'Fairly dark and sinister stuff. Horror stories, gruesome murder mysteries, that kind of thing. A few big ghost stories.'

'Well, he lived in a creepy old house,' she said with a shudder. 'I can see where he got his inspiration.' She took another bite of her burger.

I shrugged. 'Doesn't seem to be rubbing off on me, unfortunately.'

'Still having trouble with your latest book?'

'Yeah,' I nodded glumly.

That seemed to kill the conversation and we sat in silence for a while, both nibbling on our food, until Lisa decided to break the silence.

'So have you met many of the locals yet?' she asked.

'Not many. My nearest neighbour – Maddy – introduced herself yesterday, brought me some wine and flowers.' I smiled as I said this.

'Giving you gifts already? Does she have a crush on you then?' teased my daughter.

'No, it's not like that,' I said, but I started to flush slightly as I said it.

'You've got a crush on *her*, haven't you!' exclaimed Lisa under her breath. 'I can tell by the look on your face.'

'It's not like that... I barely know her,' I said, but Lisa wasn't having any of it.

'You do though, don't you?' she insisted.

I gave an almost unnoticeable shrug. 'Maybe. She seemed very nice.'

'Pretty?'

I smiled and gave a small nod. Just thinking about her face brought a smile to mine.

'Well, when are you going to ask her out then?'

'It's not that simple, Lisa.'

'Does she like you?'

I shrugged. 'I guess so. As far as I can tell.'

'Then it *is* that simple.'

'Lisa...'

'Look,' she interrupted. 'If it's about mum, then you need to get it straight in your head. It's over, dad. You're not going to get back together again. This isn't some cheesy soap opera where you keep divorcing and then getting back with your ex. I've seen her with Rupert. She's happy, dad – happier than she'd been with you for quite some time.'

I sighed. I supposed she was right. Part of me had been holding on to the memories of my wife. My *ex*-wife, I reminded myself again. But a larger part of me knew that it was never going to happen.

'You need to move on,' said Lisa, as if she knew what I was thinking. 'She's happier now...and you have a right to be happy too.'

'I suppose you're right,' I acknowledged.

'You'll ask her out?'

'I'll think about it,' I conceded. 'What about you? Have you got a new boyfriend in your life yet?'

'Ugh,' she moaned. 'Don't talk to me about teenage boys. They're all such idiots.'

As we finished our food and drank our way through several soft drinks, we carried on with idle chit-chat that gradually grew into a long hard chat about how our lives were going. It was always a relief when Lisa confirmed that her life was still on track, despite all the obstacles that my wife and I – my *ex*-wife and I – had thrown in her way.

By the time we arrived back at Lake View Cottage, it was late. Lisa was tired and decided that it was time for her to go to bed. After our long conversation, I was feeling happy for a change, and didn't want to sour my mood by staying up late and failing to write yet again, so I decided to join her in an early night.

I was deep asleep, dreaming soundly of better times, when I awoke suddenly, startled back to consciousness by a blood-curdling scream.

'Lisa?' I yelled, jumping out of bed and stumbling to the door on legs that hadn't woken as quickly as the rest of me. I pulled it open just as Lisa burst out of her bedroom on the other side of the landing. 'What is it?' I cried. She was shaking, her face white and pale.

She said nothing and I rushed past her, bursting into the room. The light was on and there was no sign of anything out of the ordinary. I turned back to my daughter. 'What is it?' I asked again.

'There was...someone in there with me,' she said between huge gulps of air, tears running down her face.

'Who? Where?' I stepped back into her bedroom. There was no other door and the only opening window was small and shut. Unlikely as it was, I opened the wardrobe and checked under the bed, but there was no one there. There was nowhere else to hide.

'A wo-woman,' she stuttered from where she stood on the landing, peering back at me around the door frame. 'In the corner of the room.'

I took a couple of steps towards the far corner just to double check, but I couldn't see whatever had spooked her. There was nothing out of the ordinary in here, just as I had known there wouldn't be.

'What did you see?' I asked softly, stepping back to my daughter and taking her in my arms. 'Tell me.'

'I got up to go to the toilet,' she said. 'I didn't turn the light on as I was still half asleep. I'd come back to my room and climbed into bed when I heard...' Her voice trailed off, as if too scared to continue.

'Heard what, honey?'

'I don't know,' she whispered back at me. 'It was like a low hiss. I turned to look and there was a woman. A woman standing in the shadows in the corner of my room.'

'A woman?'

'I know how it sounds. I know what you think.'

'I don't think anything,' I said, trying to sound reassuring but probably failing. 'Just tell me what happened.'

'I jumped out of bed, scrambling towards the door, where I flicked the light on. When I turned back...she was gone.'

'Lisa,' I began slowly. 'It was just your imagination.'

'I know what I saw, dad.'

'But honey...,' I started. 'Listen to yourself. You said yourself that this place gave you the creeps. You were half asleep. It must have just been the shadows. The moonlight coming in through the windows, especially with all those trees out there – it can cast funny shadows.'

She shook her head, but I just gave her another hug, holding her tight. 'I know it seemed real at the time, but think about it. There's no one in there. *Look.*'

She hesitated, and then turned, stepping back to the doorway and peering in.

'Come on,' I said, as I led her back into her room. 'You'll look at this all differently in the morning after some sleep.' I sat down on her bed and managed to get her to sit down next to me, although she was reluctant at first.

'There's no way I'm going to be able to get back to sleep again,' she said.

I looked at my watch; it was almost two in the morning. 'You're going to have to try. Look, read a book for a bit or something until you calm down again. You'll be fine, I promise.'

'Okay,' she said. She had stopped crying now and was starting to look calm again. 'Can you leave the landing light on?'

'Okay,' I said, with a sympathetic nod.

I stood up and she shuffled over, picking up the novel she had been reading and slipping under the duvet. The book looked like it was a horror story with some kind of monster on the cover. That was probably what had given her nightmares.

'Dad?' she called out to me as I left.

'Yes?'

'Can you leave the door open a crack?'

I nodded, leaving it ajar a couple of inches as I pulled it to behind me and returned to my own bed.

Chapter 6

The next morning, I was downstairs in the kitchen making myself some breakfast when Lisa plodded in. From the look of her, she had only just woken up. She was still in her pyjamas, her hair tousled and with sleep still in the corner of her eye.

'How are you feeling?' I asked, trying my best to sound sympathetic without sounding patronizing.

'A bit better. Took me a while to get back to sleep though.'

'Did you sleep okay in the end?'

'Not great. I spent most of the night tossing and turning.'

I took a sip of my coffee.

'Thanks for the pendant though,' she added as an afterthought, as she lumbered over towards the toaster to make herself some toast.

'Pendant?' I asked, an expression of incomprehension spread across my face.

'The one you left at the foot of my bed last night, after I'd gone back to bed,' she said. As if to explain she reached under the neck of her top and pulled out a small silver pendant on a chain. 'It's lovely. Thanks, dad.' She came over, giving me a small peck on the cheek.

I didn't have the heart to tell her that I had no idea where it came from. Maybe it had been left in the room by a previous occupant, maybe a secret admirer had hidden it in one of her bags before she came up here, although how it came to be on her bed I had no idea.

'Can I have another look at it?' I said. 'By daylight?'

She held it up for me to look at, and I peered closer. It was roughly circular, about half an inch across, a set of interconnected silver curves in an intricate pattern. 'It suits you,' I said.

'Is the kettle boiled?' she asked.

'Pretty much,' I said. 'Help yourself to coffee.'

After lunch, I collapsed onto the sofa to watch some TV while Lisa went upstairs to have a hot bath and relax. The weather outside was worsening, with dark clouds obscuring the sky and the rain falling hard, streaks of water trickling down the windows.

The air from the central heating was warm and stuffy, and I was finding it harder and harder to focus on the television, my eyelids growing heavy. I was just starting to drift in and out of consciousness when I heard a loud bang from upstairs, instantly bringing me back to my senses. Then there was a scream. I half rolled, half fell off the sofa, picking myself up from my hands and knees and clambering up the stairs.

What had started as a single bang was now a frantic hammering, which grew louder and more distraught as I reached the landing. It was coming from the bathroom door and as I grabbed the handle and twisted it, the door opened. Lisa flew out, falling into my open arms and almost knocking me over.

'Oh dad!' she cried.

'What? What is it?' She was clearly distressed.

'I... I...' she stuttered. She was crying, and shaking so badly that she could barely speak.

'Calm down,' I said soothingly, holding her tight. 'What is it? Whatever it was, it's over now.' Behind her, the room looked dark and wet. The light was off, but by the light coming in from the window and hallway, the floor and walls looked damp. There was no sign of any movement.

Lisa took a couple of deep breaths. 'There was someone in there, dad.'

Not this again, I thought, but didn't say out loud. 'It was just your imagination,' I said, calmly and patiently. Letting go of her for a moment, I stepped inside and looked around again. I pulled the cord to turn on the light but nothing happened; the bulb must have blown. 'There's no one there, Lisa.'

'There was,' she insisted. 'I was in the bath when the lights suddenly went out. I climbed out, wrapping myself in a towel to keep warm and went to pull the cord, but nothing happened. Then...there was someone in there with me, dad. In the darkness. I tried to open the door, but it wouldn't open...even when I'd drawn back the lock.'

'You saw someone in there with you?'

'Well, no,' she admitted.

'Heard them, then?'

'No. I could just sense them,' she said, a faraway look in her eyes. 'Don't look at me like that,' she said when she saw the look on my face.

'You must have still been spooked after last night. It was just your imagination playing tricks on you in the dark.'

'I didn't just imagine it. What about the door?'

I knew the door couldn't have been locked. It had opened as soon as I had turned the handle.

'I don't know,' I said with a sigh. 'Maybe you were twisting the handle the wrong way in panic. From the moisture all over the wall and floor, you must have been having one hell of a hot bath. Maybe the moisture and condensation caused your hands to slip, or the wood to warp and the door to get stuck.'

'And the light?'

'The bulb's blown, that's all. Just an unhappy coincidence – it happens all the time. Look, I'll change the bulb and then call the letting company to get them to check the door.'

'I want to go,' she said. 'I need to go home. Now,' she added, storming off towards her room.

'Honey...' I started, but she had already slammed the door shut behind her.

❉   ❉   ❉

There was a business card for the letting company pinned to the fridge door with a magnet, and I pulled it free, slipping my mobile from my pocket and dialling their number.

'Good afternoon, Alpire Letting, how can I help you?' came a female voice that sounded elderly and well educated.

'Hi, this is Peter Banner. I'm currently renting a cottage from you, Lake View Cottage in Treleven. I just moved in a few days ago.'

There was the sound of fingers hitting keys as she typed the details into a computer. 'And how can I help you today, Mr Banner?'

'It's a small thing really, but the bathroom door appears to be sticking shut sometimes. My daughter got stuck in there earlier, and couldn't get out until I opened the door from the outside.'

'I'm sorry to hear that, Mr Banner. Would you like me to send an engineer out?'

'That would be great.'

A few more taps on the keyboard. 'You're in luck. An engineer is already booked to visit another nearby property tomorrow. We should be able to have him swing by when he's finished.'

'That's great. My daughter will be going back to stay with her mother shortly, and I'll be on my own tonight. I can leave the door open for now.'

I could hear more clicks as she rapidly typed the details into the computer.

'If you're not around when he calls, is it okay if the engineer lets himself in?'

'Yeah, that should be fine.'

'Okay, that's all booked. Is there anything else I can help you with today?' she asked politely.

'No, that's it.'

I said my goodbyes, and then hung up the phone, slipping it back into my pocket. When I looked up, Lisa was standing in the hallway, bag in hand.

'Can we go now?'

* * *

The atmosphere in the car on her journey home was frosty, Lisa barely saying a word. I wasn't sure whether she was simply angry with me or still shaken by her experience. When we arrived back at her house, I just stopped outside and she grabbed her bags and ran in.

'Love you. See you again soon!' I called after her as she hurried up the drive, but if she heard me, she didn't reply.

By the time I had returned back to Lake View Cottage, the rain had deteriorated again into a full-blown storm that was pelting against the windows and causing the trees in the garden to sway sickeningly.

I hurried back into the house with my collar turned up to keep out the rain, locking the car as I ran. Once inside, I slipped off my damp shoes and removed my coat before I turned the lights on. As I bent down to pick up my shoes, I spied a small piece of paper lying near the front door. I leant over to pick it up, revealing it to be a small handwritten note, folded in half. It was from Maddy, explaining that she had called round while I was out, but she would try again tomorrow. She didn't say why she had called.

I put the note down on the table next to the door and headed straight to the whisky, pouring myself a stiff drink and almost downing it in a single gulp. *God damn it*, I thought to myself. *Why does nothing with my family ever work out how it should?* I'd hoped Lisa would like it here, and I would see more of her. Now I'd be lucky to ever get her to set foot in this place again. I still had almost three months on the lease.

I refilled my glass, this time adding a small amount of water, before sitting down at the dining room table and opening up my laptop. I just wanted to try and bury myself in my writing and forget about the weekend and the worsening relationship with my daughter.

As the evening turned into night, however, I simply grew more frustrated and angry; I still couldn't manage to write anything of any substance. As the hours went by, the only thing that was progressing with any satisfaction was the level of my inebriation. I was sitting in the darkness, the glow of the laptop screen and the occasional flash of lightning my only illumination, when I noticed the time in the corner of the screen: it was past two in the morning.

I stood up, knocking the chair backwards onto the ground and almost falling over after it. The room was slowly spinning before my eyes and I staggered across the room and up the stairs to the bathroom. Once I had relieved myself, I shuffled over to my bedroom, undoing my belt and letting my trousers fall to the floor before I flopped forwards onto the bed and fell asleep almost instantly.

I had the dream again that night.

I found myself standing on the patio behind Lake View Cottage once more, facing the house with the lake behind me. I shivered as a cool breeze blew over my flesh – or was there more to it than that?

The sun was bright and low, not long after sunrise, and I moved towards the house, reaching out to the bay doors and pulling them slowly open. As I stepped through and into the house, I could see that the inside was almost meticulously neat and tidy, the old-fashioned typewriter still sitting on the table next to a pile of paper.

A sheet of paper was protruding from the top of the typewriter, several short paragraphs visible. I wanted to go over and look at what was written, but I couldn't. I could feel that something was desperately wrong here; I could feel it in my bones, goosebumps running across my arms.

Instead of the table, I found myself being drawn towards the stairs and whatever lay at the top of them. I paused at the bottom and could feel my heart beating in my chest.

As I lifted my leg up onto the first step, I began to hear the sound of running water from upstairs. Almost upon hearing the sound, my legs felt heavier than normal, as if I was wearing leaden shoes. The first floor seemed far away and distant – a ridiculous number of steps away – but I started anyway. Step by step, I slowly plodded up the stairs, never seeming to make any progress. I felt like I had walked for hours, but every time I looked up, the landing seemed no closer.

Chapter 7

I awoke roughly, with a monstrous headache and a ringing between my ears. No, I thought to myself as the ringing stopped. It was something else; it was the doorbell.

I swung my legs out of bed and stood up on shaky legs. 'I'm coming,' I called out as I pulled a dressing gown over my shoulders and picked up my watch. It was almost one in the afternoon. How had I slept in so late?

I stumbled down the stairs, still half asleep, and opened the door to find a man in overalls carrying a toolbox – presumably the engineer that the letting company had promised.

'Hi, I'm from Alpire Letting,' said the main, confirming my assumption. 'Something about a stuck door?'

I nodded and grunted an acknowledgement.

'Late night?' asked the engineer, looking me up and down.

'Something like that,' I said, stepping back and letting him into the house.

'I'm sorry if I woke you,' he added.

I shook my head. 'No need to apologize. It's...' I looked at my watch again. 'It's almost one. I should have been up hours ago.' I stifled a brief yawn. 'I need a coffee when I get up before I'm human. Do you want one?'

'I'm fine for now – just had one on the way over.'

'Do you need me to show you the door?'

'Main bathroom?'

I nodded.

'I know the way,' he said.

'My daughter said she couldn't open it, no matter how hard she tried.'

'And it wasn't just locked by mistake?'

'I can't say for certain, but it opened as soon as I tried from the outside, so I can't see how.'

'Okay, I'll go and have a look.'

He plodded upstairs with his toolbox as I took a step into the kitchen and put some water in the kettle. As it boiled, I caught my reflection in the window: unshaven, hair dishevelled, sullen eyes. I'd have to freshen myself up, just as soon as he'd finished in there.

It was about ten minutes later, the caffeine just starting to kick in, when I heard him coming down the stairs. I wandered into the hallway to find him putting his toolbox on the floor next to the front door.

'All done?' I asked.

He shrugged. 'Couldn't find anything wrong with it, I'm afraid.'

'Oh,' I said. 'I guess it must have just been Lisa panicking. Maybe the handle had been slippery from moisture.'

'I replaced the lock anyway, just to be sure,' he added. 'You're quite isolated out here, and if you're living on your own you really don't want to get stuck in there if you can help it.'

'That's great,' I said with an appreciative smile. 'Thanks.'

'Not a problem. Now that I've replaced the lock I doubt it'll happen again, but if it does, just let us know.'

'Will do,' I said with a nod.

After having a bite to eat, I decided to go for a walk. I needed to try and clear my mind and banish my hangover.

The storm had dissipated considerably from the previous night, although there was still a strong wind, and I put on my best walking boots, wrapping up tight with a scarf and winter jacket before heading out of the house.

I walked around the wood and started up the hill, Maddy's house coming into view again. For a moment I continued walking along the path and then stopped, wondering about going up and knocking on her door to say hello. As I stood there thinking, Maddy suddenly appeared, standing up from behind the garden's dry stone wall. She was holding a trowel in one hand, and I guessed she had been doing some gardening. She glanced around, noticing me standing on the path and looking at her. Then she waved me over.

'Doing some weeding?' I asked as I drew close, desperately trying to find some small talk.

'Just planting some new bulbs,' she said. 'I've had them for ages, and have kept putting it off... What?'

I realized I had been staring at her. She had a smudge of dirt on the tip of her nose that had caught my attention.

'Nothing. It's just...' I stammered awkwardly. 'Just a bit of dirt,' I added as I raised a finger to her face and brushed the soil from the end of her nose.

She said nothing, but the edges of her mouth raised slightly with an embarrassed grin, a slight flush coming to her cheeks – or was that just the cold wind?

'Would you like a coffee?' she asked after a few moments of uncomfortable silence. 'Or tea?'

'A coffee would be great,' I said, perhaps a bit too eagerly.

'I was just finishing up anyway,' she said, picking up a mat and gloves from the floor.

'Let me take those for you,' I offered awkwardly, but she batted my offer away.

'I'm fine – and you don't know where they go anyway.'

I nodded and followed her as she turned and headed back to the house. Once inside, she proceeded to remove her muddy boots and coat, and I followed her lead, untying my walking boots and putting them on a mat by the front door.

Maddy gesticulated towards the open doorway of the living room. 'Make yourself at home, while I go and clean up.'

I removed my coat, hanging it up on an empty peg by the front door, and stepped into the lounge. It was a quiet, restrained room. Several bookshelves lined one wall, although they were covered more by ornaments and mementoes than books. There was a modest-sized television in front of the window and a leather sofa facing it, two armchairs on either side. A framed watercolour sat on one wall: the view of the village from the top of the hill.

From a distance, it looked quite good, and the quality didn't diminish as I came in for a closer inspection. I checked the signature in the corner to confirm that it was indeed one of Maddy's; I wasn't sure why she had been so embarrassed when the subject of her paintings had been brought up the other day.

I stood for a moment by the window, looking out at the now-familiar landscape beyond. From here, the lake was still just about visible in the distance, extending off towards the horizon. I didn't want to appear too nosy, and so decided to sit down in one of the armchairs. As I sat scanning the room, I noticed a small brown parcel on the coffee table next to me – a package from Amazon, one side ripped open.

I knew I shouldn't, that it was incredibly rude, but I couldn't help myself. Professional curiosity got the better of me, and I picked it up, reaching inside to pull out the contents. My hunch was correct; it was one of my novels – my first novel in fact. I could feel a cheeky grin on my face as I slipped it back into the packet and placed it back on the table.

'How do you take it?' came a voice suddenly, making me almost jump out of my seat. I turned to see Maddy standing in the doorway.

'I'm sorry?' I spluttered.

'Your coffee,' she said, with a look of slight bemusement on her face. 'How do you take it?'

'Oh. Black, no sugar.'

She turned and headed back towards the kitchen. If she'd noticed me peeking at her mail, she'd been too polite to say anything – or just maybe I had got away with it. I decided to leave the scene of the crime, and stood up, following her into the kitchen.

She removed a white mug from a coffee machine and handed it to me, before replacing it with one for herself. I waited patiently while the machine hissed and spat hot coffee into her mug.

'Are you settled in yet?' she asked, once she had taken a sip of her drink.

'Pretty much,' I said. 'I'm all unpacked, almost used to the place. My daughter, not so much.'

'Oh?'

'She came down for the weekend, but hated the place. She said it gave her the creeps, and had a couple of bad experiences.'

'What do you mean by bad experiences?'

'Oh, nothing really. She had a bad nightmare in the night, and I think she then just let her imagination get the better of her.'

'How old is she?'

'Sixteen. Doing her GCSEs in the summer. She's back home again with her mother now – I don't know if I'll ever convince her to come back here again,' I said with a sigh.

Maddy nodded, as if deep in thought, but didn't reply.

'You left me a note yesterday,' I said. 'When I was out.'

'Oh yes,' she said, coming back to the moment. 'I was wondering if you wanted to come over to dinner tonight. You must be very lonely on your own – I assume you don't know anyone else round here?'

I shook my head. 'Bumped into a couple of locals, but you're the only person I've actually had a proper chat with. I was actually planning to ask you if you wanted to come to dinner at *my* house tonight, to repay you for the wine and flowers.'

'That sounds wonderful,' she said. 'What time?'

'How about seven?'

'It's a date.'

And there it was. My first date in almost twenty years.

It had gone seven, and I was already pacing up and down in the kitchen, my stomach a bundle of nerves. I glanced at my watch again. It was only five past; she was barely late at all.

I'd already opened a bottle of red wine to let it air, and I was taking another sip from my glass to try and ease my nerves when the doorbell rang. I jumped, almost dropping the glass and cursing to myself under my breath.

I put the glass down and took a couple of deep breaths before heading to the front door. It seemed further away than I remembered. I opened the door to find Maddy looking radiant in a dark blue dress. She was holding a bottle of wine in one hand, and in the other was something large, which I couldn't quite make out in the darkness.

'Come in,' I said. 'You must be freezing.'

'Not too bad,' she said. 'I drove over on account of this.' She held out the item in her left hand, showing it to be a rectangular parcel roughly two feet square and wrapped in brown paper.

I took it from her graciously, and she could obviously see the look of bewilderment on my face. 'It's a housewarming present,' she said. 'But something to open after dinner. This is for before,' she added, holding up the bottle of wine.

I looked around for a moment for somewhere to put the parcel, deciding in the end to place it next to the coffee table in the living room.

'You look lovely,' I said, and I meant it.

'Thanks,' she replied with a smile. There seemed to be a twinkle in her eyes tonight.

We went through to the dining room. I had taken my laptop upstairs to make room for two place settings, leaving it on the desk in the blue room. Maddy took a seat at the far side of the table with her back to the wall and I filled up her wine glass, taking the opportunity to refresh mine too.

I had cooked a meal of roast salmon with crispy vegetables and a side salad – something nice but not too complicated – and we sat down to enjoy our dinner, talking about the local area and our careers, mostly just small talk, nothing too personal or intimate. When we had finished, we adjourned to the living room so that I could open her present.

'I needed you to have some wine first,' she said. 'You have to promise you won't laugh.'

'I promise,' I said as I held the package in my hands, wondering what on earth she had brought me. Then the combination of the size and light weight triggered a thought in my mind.

I carefully unwrapped the brown paper to reveal first a wooden frame, and then – as I had suspected – a watercolour painting. I pulled the rest of the paper from the frame and held it in both hands, giving it a good appraisal. It was a landscape of the sun going down over the lake, and off to the left-hand side was a cottage.

'That's this house over on the left,' said Maddy. 'I thought it might look nice in here.'

'It's good,' I said. It wasn't perfect, but the way she captured the dying sunlight reflecting off the water was quite effective.

'You're not just saying that?'

'No, and you didn't have to get me drunk first. I think I'll still appreciate it in the morning.'

'If you don't want to put it up on display, you don't have to,' she said with a little embarrassment.

'Nonsense,' I said. 'I'll hang it in the blue room.'

'The blue room?'

'Sorry, I named the rooms upstairs after their colours. It's the room that Lisa was staying in. Hopefully, it might brighten her mood next time she's down.' I took another look at the picture as I held it in my hands. It really was quite good. 'Why don't we go and hang it now?' I suggested, and she replied with a smile and a nod.

We both ascended the stairs to the blue room, Maddy following close behind me. Inside, there was a cheap print of some abstract art hanging on the wall above the bed, something left there by the letting company. I took it down and replaced it with the watercolour, standing back next to Maddy to admire it.

'The colour of the sky and the water really complement the wallpaper in here,' I said. 'It's lovely.'

'You really mean it?'

'I do,' I said as I turned to face her. I wanted to add that I thought she looked lovely too. I took a half step towards her, and she didn't back away. I thought I could see a hint of a smile forming on her lips again, a mischievous glimmer in her eyes.

I was contemplating moving closer again when the door to the room slammed shut with a bang, causing us both to jump.

'Jesus!' exclaimed Maddy.

'It must have been a gust of wind,' I said. The small window in here had been open, but I hadn't felt anything. I looked at her again. Whatever we had been feeling about each other, the moment was gone. Now it just felt like I'd lured her upstairs and trapped her in a bedroom. I stepped over to the door to open it again. 'Sorry about that,' I muttered.

'No problem, it just caught me by surprise,' she said with a shake of her head. 'I'm sorry,' she said, as she glanced at her watch, 'but it's getting late and I need to be up for work in the morning.'

I walked her back downstairs again, my heart a confusing mix of elation and dejection.

'Do you mind if I leave my car here and pick it up in the morning?' she asked. 'It's not far, but I've had a bit too much to drink really. I don't want to wrap it around one of the trees in the forest.'

'Will you be okay? I can walk you home?' I offered.

She just shook her head. 'I'm a big girl. I've wandered these lanes on my own for years. I think I can make it. I've got some sensible shoes and a coat in the boot.'

'If you're sure?'

'Yes,' she said, firmly but politely. 'But...'

'Yes?' I asked expectantly.

'I've enjoyed myself tonight, Peter. Let me return the favour by having you over for dinner tomorrow.'

'That would be lovely.'

'Seven again?'

'Perfect.'

After Maddy had left, I sat down on the sofa with a glass of whisky in my hand. I had already drunk quite a lot of wine over dinner, but I didn't care. For the first time since my divorce, I thought I actually felt happy. Not just superficially happy, but happy deep down inside. I liked Maddy – *really* liked her. I felt more for her than I had for anyone since I'd met my ex-wife, and I got the definite impression that she liked me too.

Buoyed by my mood, I stood up and finished clearing the dining room table, placing the dishes and cutlery in the dishwasher. Then I headed back upstairs to where I had left my laptop on the desk in the blue room.

I glanced at the time – it was almost midnight – and then started to write. For the first time since my divorce, I found I actually could. Maybe it was the alcohol, but I thought it more likely that it was Maddy. I might have lost my old muse, but just maybe I had found a new one.

Chapter 8

I woke up late the following morning with a dry mouth and mild headache, but also a large smile across my face. I pulled myself from the warmth of my bed and dressed before wandering down to the kitchen and making myself a strong coffee.

With that done, I wandered back upstairs and into the blue room where my laptop was still running, the glow of its screen clearly visible – I'd obviously forgotten to shut it down before going to bed. The storm seemed to have blown over and while it still looked windy, the dark clouds had gone and the sun was now streaming in through the windows.

I sat down at the desk, squinting in the bright light, and looked at my work from last night. I'd done more than I'd remembered – quite a lot more in fact – although I was having trouble remembering much apart from drinking far too much wine and whisky. I took a deep sip of my coffee as I read back through the words. *Damn*, I thought. *This is some good shit.* The prose was some of the best I had written for a while, but the more I read, the more a frown grew across my face. It was just too angry, too bitter. Despite my feelings about Maddy, my drunken state had obviously let too many of the raw emotions from my divorce bleed their way into the text, and the hatred and vitriol between Gabriel and Harriet was just too much for this novel.

I took one more read of the new paragraphs. It started off okay, but then... It just didn't work in this context; I shook my head and sighed. It was just too out of character. I'd joked to myself about divorcing my two protagonists, but I didn't think it was something I could actually do; it wasn't something any of my fans would want to read.

I hated to do it, but I selected the bulk of the additions from last night, took a deep sigh and then pressed delete, consigning it all to digital oblivion.

I spent most of the day in a giddy state, feeling like a love-struck teenager once again. The date had obviously gone well, given that Maddy had invited me over to her house for dinner again tonight. I was excited but also nervous. I was starting to get invested in the relationship already, and I didn't want to screw it up.

With excitement running through my veins I set to work on my novel again, and with a noticeable improvement. I didn't manage to write a whole lot, but I did at least manage to write, and for a nice change I was even happy with my work.

I stuck at it all day, until I glanced at my watch and noticed that it was half-past six, only half an hour until I was due round at Maddy's. I rubbed my fingers against my chin; I had almost two days' worth of stubble, and must have looked a right state. It was a while since I had showered too – I probably stank. A quick shower and a shave were clearly in order before I left, so I went up to my bedroom and found a fresh set of clothes before heading to the bathroom. There, I dug out my electric razor from of the cabinet and had a quick shave before putting the shower on. It was an old-style shower attached to the bath and fed off the same water supply, but the water was hot and the pressure good – no need for a power shower here. I waited for a few moments until the water was running nice and hot, clouds of steam billowing out where it met the cold air. Then I climbed in, scrubbing all over with soap and running some shampoo through my hair before I decided I'd done enough. It was warm and pleasant in there, but I had things to do, places to go. I climbed out, rubbing myself dry on a warm towel before getting dressed.

Once in my clothes, I stepped over to the sink to check my appearance in the mirror. The glass was covered in condensation and I ran a hand across the cold surface, wiping it clean.

As I did so, there was a quiet crack and the bathroom light cut out, plunging me into darkness. But just before the light went I caught a glimpse of a face in the mirror: a woman with long dark hair standing behind me. It was just a momentary glance before the light disappeared, and I whirled around instinctively, but I couldn't see anything in the darkness, let alone another person in there with me. I could feel a presence though. I couldn't tell you exactly what it was that I sensed, but it definitely felt like there was someone there in the blackness with me. All at once, I knew what my daughter had experienced in here to freak her out so badly, and I wished I hadn't dismissed her experiences quite so quickly.

I took a couple of steps backwards, backing into the corner of the room, away from whoever or whatever was in there with me. I only stopped when my head hit the cabinet that was mounted on the wall – not hard enough to make me cry out, but hard enough to hurt, nevertheless.

I stood in the darkness, straining my ears to hear whatever was in here with me, but there was nothing, just the distant sound of wind rushing through the trees and over the roof tiles. My heart was pounding, but part of me still wondered if I had imagined it all. Had I just imagined the face behind me as the light blew? Had it been a trick of the light, just a strange shape in the shadows?

Then it struck me how cold it was in here. Just moments ago it had been hot and steamy. I had almost been sweating when I stepped from the shower, but now I could feel the goose flesh on my arms.

I didn't know what to do, but I did know that I couldn't just stay in here. My eyes were adjusting to the darkness and could now make out the shape of the bathroom door. The landing lights weren't on outside, but there were lights on elsewhere in the house, and small amount of light was seeping in through the cracks.

I made my mind up almost instantly, and sprinted towards the exit. As I ran, I wondered about the door – would I be unable to open it, like my daughter? She had had me on the other side to open it for her, but I had no one. Would I be stuck in here? Would someone from the letting company find me in here several days from now, frozen to death, a grimace of fear on my face?

My hand grasped the door handle as I reached the other side of the room, and I frantically turned it. I hadn't bothered locking the door, but such was my level of panic, I fear that if I had I surely wouldn't have had the clarity of mind to unlock it.

As I fumbled with the handle, I felt something brushing against the back of my neck, something as light and delicate as a spider's web. Then the handle turned in my hand, and the door burst open with dim light from downstairs sweeping in. With it, the feeling at the back of my neck was gone.

I stumbled forwards, falling to my hands and knees as I clambered out of the room, turning to look behind me. All I could see was an empty bathroom, dark and deserted.

Still, I didn't stop, didn't go back to check. I grabbed the banister at the top of the stairs, dragging myself back to my feet, and made my way down the stairs as quickly as my shaking legs would let me.

I picked up my shoes from by the front door, stabbing my feet into them, not bothering with the laces. Then I opened the door with my left hand as I grabbed a jacket with my right, running through it and out onto the gravel drive outside.

Only there did I stop and turn to look at the house. It looked calm and quiet, peaceful. There were no signs of anything out of the ordinary.

I felt like I now knew where Ed Steele had got the inspiration for his ghost stories: how they had been quite so atmospheric, why they had been so successful. The man had been living in a real-life haunted house.

I also felt like a complete shit for dismissing my daughter's fears so casually.

As I stood in the cold evening air, I could feel that my heart beat was slowing now, my breathing returning to normal. I took a couple of paces backwards, not daring to take my eyes from the house. Then a couple more, then another couple. Then I turned and jogged towards Maddy's house.

By the time I reached Maddy's house and rang her doorbell, I had almost convinced the rational part of my brain that it had all just been my imagination. I had jokingly wondered about the house being haunted, and surely it had all just got to me. I was a writer, creativity was my career; weren't people like me *supposed* to have overly active imaginations? However, another part of me, a much deeper and more primal part, knew that what I had just experienced had been real.

I had considered the fact that the house might be haunted before now, toyed with the idea in my mind, but it had all been so abstract...so theoretical. Now, it felt all too real.

But then the door opened, and I was greeted by Maddy's warm face, her radiant smile, and those thoughts and feelings were pushed away, replaced by other primal emotions.

'Are you okay?' she asked.

Don't say that I look like I've seen a ghost, I thought to myself. When she just frowned some more, I managed to splutter, 'I'm fine,' with a dismissive shake of my head. 'I was just thinking about something, but it's not important.'

'Won't you come in?'

I followed her inside, back into her living room where she had two glasses of wine waiting. She handed me one and I accepted it gratefully.

'You look beautiful tonight,' I said. I wondered momentarily whether I was being a bit too forward, but I couldn't help myself; she was looking even prettier than I remembered. She was wearing a black cocktail dress that showed off her figure, and had put her hair up with some kind of fancy braids.

'Thanks,' she replied coyly, and with a slight blush of embarrassment.

'Nice wine,' I said as I took a sip, trying to change the conversation to a safer topic.

'It's just whatever was on offer at the supermarket,' she said. 'I'm afraid I don't know much about wine.'

'Me neither,' I agreed. 'I just know what I like,' I added, and it wasn't just the wine that I was referring to.

We both took another sip before she led me through to the dining room, where she had laid out two place settings, a candelabra with a trio of lighted candles in between them.

We chatted as we ate our food, our conversation deeper and more personal than the previous night; we had both became more and more comfortable opening up to each other. After we had polished off dinner and a couple of bottles of red wine, we moved to the sofa to continue our discussion in comfort.

Maddy noticed that my glass was empty, and excused herself to go to the kitchen and fetch another bottle; I didn't object. When she came back, she offered the bottle towards me and I lifted up the glass to let her refill it. Her own glass was also standing empty on a small table next to the sofa, and she topped it up next.

As she did so, my mind returned once more to what I had been trying to ignore all evening. What was waiting for me when I returned home? Was the house haunted after all? Was I even safe there?

Maddy gave me a curious glance. There had obviously been something about the look on my face.

'Penny for your thoughts?' she asked softly, as she slid back next to me on the sofa.

'I was just thinking that I really don't want to go back to my house,' I replied absent-mindedly.

'Well, aren't you forward?' she replied, mock surprise on her face.

'No,' I spluttered, 'I didn't mean it like that. I just meant...'

'Shhh,' she purred softly, as she leant forwards, placing one hand on my leg. 'I don't want you to go home either.'

Before I knew it, we were kissing. Her lips were soft but forceful, our tongues intertwining. Then I pulled away.

'What is it?' she whispered.

'I don't want to spill red wine on your sofa,' I said, gesturing to the nearly full glass in my hand. 'It would never come out.'

I turned round to place the glass on a side table, before turning back to face her. 'Now, where were we?' I said with a grin. I moved in close, kissing her again on the lips, then on the neck, on the ears. She leaned back on the sofa, pulling me down on top of her, and all thoughts of ghosts and haunted houses went from my mind.

Chapter 9

The next morning, I awoke alone in Maddy's bed. The room looked different by the morning light that was peeking in through a gap in the curtains – colder, and lacking in the warmth of the previous night.

I sat up, acutely aware that I was naked under the sheets, and set about trying to find my clothes. It didn't take me long; I was sure they had been rapidly discarded during our throes of passion, but it looked like Maddy had collected them all, neatly placing them on a chair next to the bed.

The house was still and silent, and I called out Maddy's name, but the only reply was the faint chirping of birds from outside. I quickly pulled on my clothes and then stepped out onto the landing. The house was dark, with no sign of anyone but me. I stepped cautiously down the stairs and from there into the kitchen. I was about to head for the coffee machine when I spotted a folded sheet of paper standing on the kitchen table, my name upon it. I picked it up, and found a note from Maddy, explaining that she had needed to go to work, choosing to let me sleep in rather than waking me to say goodbye. She told me to make myself at home and then lock up on my way out. She would be home later this afternoon.

I folded the paper again and slid it into my pocket before making myself that cup of coffee that I so desperately needed. With that in hand, I decided to have a quick look around – nothing nosy, but she *had* told me to make myself at home. I had a quick glance around the kitchen, at the flowers on the window sill and then at the large pile of washing up sitting in the sink, the remnants of last night's meal. I felt like I should do something nice for her, so set about washing and drying all the dirty plates and glasses, painstakingly finding the correct locations in which to put each item away. With nothing more left for me in the kitchen, I headed into the dining room. I had a quick glance around, and was about to leave when I spotted something I hadn't noticed the previous night: there was a sideboard against one wall, and on it was a solitary photograph. It was the only one I had seen anywhere in the house.

I stepped closer, picking it up to look at it more closely. It was a black and white photograph of a middle-aged man and woman standing in front of a house: *this* house. From the look of it, the picture had been taken a long time ago; this must surely be Maddy's parents, the previous owners of this house. I put it carefully back down again.

Looking around, I wondered whether Maddy would appreciate me tidying up, not that the house was particularly messy; in fact, it was pretty close to spotless.

I sighed, recognizing what I was doing. I was just trying to kill time, trying to do anything that would put off going back to my house again. I couldn't put it off forever, though. I needed to face up to it, before my fears started to consume me.

I stepped over to the front door, picking up my coat from where it hung next to the door, and put it on. Then I left, locking the door behind me.

I took the path back to Lake View Cottage, walking slowly and reluctantly, subconsciously trying to delay the inevitable. As I drew close, I stopped in the driveway and looked at the building. It all looked perfectly normal, just regular bricks and mortar standing before me in the hazy morning sunlight.

My eyes scanned the building up and down until I stopped suddenly, staring at a first-floor window. In the shadows, I could just make out a shape. It might have been a trick of the light or an odd reflection, but just for a moment it looked like the face of a woman standing a foot or two behind the glass, a gaunt face looking back at me. Then I blinked and it was gone, and all I could see were shadows.

Maybe it's not time to return to the house just yet, I thought with a shiver, instead turning and heading back down the path towards the village.

The weather was decidedly warmer than the previous day, almost to the point where I wished I hadn't worn a coat. As I crested the hill and headed down into the village, I was starting to work up a sweat. Before long, I reached the church grounds, once more taking the shortcut through the graveyard and around to the front of the church. I was strolling along at a pace, thinking about the face I had seen in the window, when a side door opened in front of me, and I had to come to a sudden halt to avoid colliding with it. The appearance of the door was quickly followed by the vicar from behind it.

'Oh, I'm so sorry,' said the vicar apologetically when he suddenly realized I was there.

'Not at all, it was entirely my fault,' I said. 'I should have been paying more attention.'

'Just as long as I didn't hit you.'

'No,' I said with a shake of my head. 'I've not sure I've introduced myself,' I added. 'I'm Peter Banner. I've just moved into Lake View Cottage, just over the hill.'

The vicar nodded as if trying to remember something. 'That's stood empty for quite a while,' he said a moment later. 'Decades, I think.'

I nodded. 'It used to belong to the author Ed Steele.'

'That's right,' said the vicar, as old memories surfaced in his mind. 'Didn't he move out after some kind of incident?'

'Incident? What kind of thing?'

'Can't say I remember. It all happened such a long time ago, more than a decade before I took over this parish, if memory serves. I just remember some idle gossip among the villagers.'

This was definitely piquing my curiosity. 'Can you remember what?'

He shook his head. 'Not really. And I'm not sure I should be spreading idle gossip and rumours anyway.'

'Oh, no,' I said. 'Sorry. I wasn't thinking.'

'No problem,' replied the vicar with a pleasant smile that I was sure he had used often.

'Oh. Yes,' I said, starting to blush. 'Well, many thanks.'

'Not at all,' he said, 'and I hope to see you next Sunday morning.'

'Oh, yes,' I said. 'I may not be around', I added with embarrassment. 'I may have to go and pick up my daughter – my wife and I are separated.' I felt strangely ashamed to admit that I hadn't stepped foot in a church for almost twenty years, not since my wedding.

'Well, if you ever feel in need of spiritual guidance, we have evening sermons too.'

'I'll bear that in mind,' I said, with a smile that felt much too fake. 'But I really must be going.'

As I reached the centre of town, I still didn't feel ready to return to the cottage just yet. Instead, I headed to the village pub for a drink and some lunch.

The Eight Bells was a small establishment just off the high street. At half-past eleven on a weekday, it was understandably quiet, with just a couple of locals sitting in one corner nursing their drinks. I ordered a pint of the guest beer and a ploughman's, settling in by the window.

Despite the lack of business – or maybe because of it – the food didn't take long to arrive. As I ate, I sat by the window watching the world go by. I was running the events from the house through my mind, trying to decide what to do. It didn't take me long to reach a conclusion: I needed to talk to Maddy about all of this. She would have grown up here when the cottage was still occupied. Maybe she would know something about it. Maybe there had been stories or rumours; not many kids grow up living next to a haunted house.

With the decision made, I already felt like some of the weight had been lifted from my chest. I wouldn't head straight back to Lake View Cottage; instead, I'd head directly to Maddy's to speak to her there – just after I'd had another pint for courage.

When I arrived back on her doorstep, the house was quiet and dark. I tried knocking on the door anyway, but as I had suspected, there was no reply. Maddy had said that she would be back in the afternoon – as opposed to the evening – but I didn't know exactly when. A quick glance at my watch confirmed that it had only just gone two o'clock. It was a nice afternoon, however, the rays of sunlight providing a gentle warmth despite the wind, and so I decided to wait for her here. There was a bench in the garden and it seemed like a nice place to sit in the sun.

I didn't have to wait long. Just before half-past, her old Golf pulled into the driveway. As she got out, I could see a confused look on her face.

'What's wrong?' she called as she walked over. 'Locked yourself out of your house?'

'No,' I said with a cheesy grin on my face. 'Just couldn't wait to see you again.'

'Now I know something's up,' she said with a slight giggle. 'What's the matter?'

'I just need to talk to you about something,' I said.

Maddy paused momentarily and turned to face me. 'Sounds serious,' she said with a raised eyebrow, before resuming her walk to the front door.

I ambled along next to her. 'Not really,' I said, with a shrug of my shoulders that I hoped looked more nonchalant then it felt. 'Just some local history really.'

Maddy unlocked the front door and stepped inside, holding the door open for me. I followed her inside, removing my shoes and coat. We moved into the living room, settling down next to each other on the sofa.

'I've got to say I'm glad to see you again so soon,' she said as soon as we were seated. 'I... well, I enjoyed your company last night.' I could see her cheeks were flushed and she couldn't quite look me in the eye.

'You've nothing to feel embarrassed about,' I replied. 'I enjoyed last night too.'

She let out a little giggle. 'I know you did, by the way you–'

'–What I meant was... I enjoyed being with you.'

Maddy raised a single eyebrow and gave me a knowing smile. It made me suddenly realize just how much I already cared for her.

'I didn't mean that. Not that I didn't enjoy that,' I spluttered. I stopped and took a breath to compose myself. 'I'm trying to say that I enjoyed having dinner with you, talking with you. Just being in your company.'

She flashed me a wide smile and placed one hand on mine. 'I enjoyed it too. Now what was it you wanted to talk to me about? I'm sure it wasn't just last night.'

'I want to talk to you about Lake View Cottage.'

'Okay. What about it?'

'You've lived here all your life. Were there ever any rumours about the place? Any stories?'

'Stories? Like what?'

'I don't know. Rumours of odd occurrences, or strange things happening.'

'Well, no. But no one's lived there for almost thirty years. I'm not quite sure what you're after.'

'Well, I'm thinking of back when Ed Steele used to live there. Do you remember anything unusual?'

'How old do you think I am?' she chuckled. 'You have to remember that I was only five or six when they left. I've only got some very vague memories from back then.'

I took a deep breath. This was where I'd find out whether she thought I was bat-shit crazy or not. 'I've seen some weird stuff since I moved in.'

She gave me a curious look. 'What do you mean *weird*?'

'Unexplained noises. A couple of times I thought I saw something in the house... some*one*.'

'It sounds like you're just getting used to a new house. A new house that's pretty old, if you know what I mean.'

'It's more than just that,' I said, grimacing slightly as I did so. 'This isn't just a few creaks at night, the odd weird shadow or two. My daughter got stuck in the bathroom, and was sure that there was someone in there with her.'

'But there *wasn't*... right?'

'Not as far as I could tell.'

'So what did you tell your daughter?'

I sighed. 'The same thing you're telling me now. That it was just an unfamiliar house. Just her imagination playing tricks on her. But...'

'But?'

'Yesterday, before I came over to see you, I experienced something... I felt something. It wasn't just tricks of the light and an overactive imagination. There was *something* in that house with me.'

'So what are you trying to tell me?'

'I think the house is haunted.' There; I had said it.

'*Haunted*?' She sounded very sceptical, as I supposed she had every right to be.

'I know how it sounds. I'd feel exactly the same as you if I hadn't experienced it myself. Hell, I *did* feel exactly the same as you when something happened to my daughter.'

Maddy sat in silence for a moment. 'So what are you going to do?'

'Come and have dinner with me again at Lake View Cottage,' I suggested. 'See if you witness anything yourself or if you think I'm just going mad. And if it's not too presumptuous, spend the night there.'

She chuckled, a wide grin on her face. 'And there we have it... your true motive.'

'It's not like that,' I smiled back. 'I have spare rooms.'

She leaned forwards and gave me a kiss on the cheek. 'I think I'll be fine,' she whispered in my ear seductively. Then she leaned back slowly, reclining back down on the sofa. There was a look on her face of deep thought.

'We could be ghost hunters!' she exclaimed suddenly.

'Well... if you like,' I agreed uncertainly. 'You're not afraid?'

'I've been through enough shit in my life that this should pale by comparison. Besides, outside of Hollywood movies, I don't think ghosts can actually hurt you. Not that I've ever heard of anyone *actually* interacting with a ghost – but I'm pretty sure that even in those dodgy ghost documentaries on TV, no one's ever been attacked by one.'

The look on her face changed back to pensive thought again before another thought burst forth. 'Ed Steele!' she exclaimed. 'Do you think that's where he got his ideas from? The plots for all of his novels?'

I nodded. 'As a matter of fact, I do.'

'Well, maybe your agent was right. Maybe the cottage *will* inspire you like it inspired him!'

'If it doesn't scare me to death first. Ed must have had a stronger stomach than me.'

'Until you arrived, it had been thirty years since anyone spent a night in that house. If the place *is* haunted, the ghost has presumably been alone all that time. If you left me alone for thirty years, I'd get pretty fucked up. Who knows how the ghost has changed over all those years?'

'You're telling me that a ghost got lonely? Five minutes ago, you were ridiculing the idea of it being haunted at all.'

She just shrugged.

'So you'll come over?' I asked.

She nodded. 'Sure, why not.'

I stood up. 'Shall I see you at about seven?'

She smiled. 'It's a date.'

I left Maddy's and headed back to the cottage, but didn't go in. I didn't want to be in there on my own any more than I had to. Instead, I got in my car and headed off to the nearest town with a decent-sized supermarket to stock up for dinner.

I returned just before five, leaving myself only two hours on my own in which to tidy up and prepare dinner. I kept telling myself that I would be fine, that it was only two hours in a house where I had already spent over a week. Still, as I opened the front door, my nerves were on edge, adrenaline coursing through my veins.

I paused in the hallway, my hands full of shopping bags, straining to hear anything, but the house was cold, dark and silent. I headed into the kitchen, dumping the food on the counter and then started to turn on all the lights, trying to banish the shadows and with them, my fears.

As time gradually drew on and nothing happened, my anxiety slowly decreased, and when Maddy arrived bang on seven o'clock, I was almost approaching calmness, although a couple of glasses of red wine may have helped.

I took her coat as she came in, and we immediately settled into a friendly and relaxed conversation, with last night's activities having banished most of the nervous tension that we'd previously felt between us.

Over dinner, we chatted about small things, neither of us really wanting to bring up the subject of the house being haunted. I think we were both nervous about what might happen tonight, and didn't want to jinx anything.

'So did you say you'd lived your whole life in your house?' I asked as I was clearing away the dishes.

'Yep,' she said as she sat at the dining room table, nursing the last remnants of her glass of wine. 'Ever since I was born in...' She giggled slightly. 'Well, ever since I was born anyway. It was my parent's house before me.'

'And they died over a decade ago, I think you said,' I called back from the kitchen, where I was stacking the plates in the dishwasher.

'Yes,' she said. 'My dad died in early 2006 from a heart attack. My mum passed a few months later. I don't think she really wanted to go on after he'd left us.'

I returned from the kitchen with another bottle of white wine. 'Top up?' Maddy nodded, and I removed the lid, refilling both of our glasses. 'And you've lived there alone ever since?'

'Not always alone,' said Maddy. 'For a couple of years I was with someone: Michael. We were engaged to be married, but...' Her voice trailed off, and she had a faraway gaze in her eyes.

We both jumped as there was a loud bang from somewhere upstairs, making me spill a few drops of wine and bringing Maddy back to the moment.

'What was that?' she asked nervously.

'I don't know,' I said. It had sounded like a door slamming shut.

Glass of wine in hand, I stood up and headed out into the hallway, Maddy close behind. I looked up the stairs towards the landing, which was shrouded in shadows. They were banished instantly as Maddy flicked the light switch behind me. There was no one visible up there, no signs of any movement.

Slowly, I climbed the stairs, Maddy by my side. On the landing, all the doors stood open or ajar but one: the master bedroom. I stood a step towards it, stopping just in front. 'Shall I?' I asked. Maddy nodded back nervously.

I grasped the door handle and twisted it, the door opening easily. A cold draught of air swept out as it swung into the room, causing Maddy to gasp. I stepped inside.

The room was dark, and looked how I remembered it when I had left, except... one of the windows was open, a cold wind blowing in.

'I must have left the window open when I came down,' I said. I was trying to remember if I had opened it or not. I supposed I must have.

'The wind must have blown the door shut,' agreed Maddy.

Standing in the darkness, I turned around to face her, taking another large swig of wine. She was standing illuminated in the doorway, looking radiant.

'So...' I said, thinking back to the conversation we had been having downstairs. 'Is your finance still around? Do I have any jealous exes to worry about?' I added with a nervous smile.

'No,' she said with a shake of her head. Something about the look on her face told me that I should drop the subject. She took a step towards me, downing the rest of her wine and placing the glass on the dresser next to her. Then she took another step towards me, so that our bodies were almost touching, and wrapped her arms around me. 'You're the only man in my life,' she purred up at me. She pushed me backwards, so that we both fell onto the double bed together. My glass, still half full of wine, tumbled to the floor, but I was beyond caring.

I awoke in darkness. It was still the middle of the night, with just a few rays of moonlight coming in through the window.

I rolled over to face Maddy who lay asleep next to me, naked under the sheets. But even in the near darkness, I could see something was wrong. Badly wrong. I reached out to touch her, and her skin felt cold and clammy, like a dead fish.

I frantically rolled over, grabbing at the switch for the bedside light and turning it on. Turning back to face Maddy, I let out an involuntary scream. Her face was pale and blue, her cold lifeless eyes staring back at me.

Then there was another scream; distant at first and then suddenly growing nearer. I jerked awake in the darkness to find Maddy sitting upright next to me. She was in tears, taking huge gulps of air.

'Are you okay?' I called frantically, almost shouting. I still had the image of her cold dead face in my mind.

'No, I'm not,' she cried, rolling out of bed, wiping the tears from her face with her arm. 'I thought I could stay here... but I can't. I can't stay another minute.' She started picking up her underwear from the floor and putting it on.

'What is it?' I asked as I climbed out of bed, grabbing a dressing gown from where it was lying on a chair next to the bed and putting it on. 'What happened?'

Maddy bent over and picked up her dress from the floor, lifting it up over her head and putting it on.

'I... I...' she stuttered. Whatever it was, she was clearly shaken.

I walked around the bed to her, gently putting my hands on her shoulders. She flinched momentarily, almost instinctively, but didn't resist. I crouched down slightly to look her directly in the eyes. 'What happened to you? What did you see?'

Her breathing was slowing slightly now. 'I guess it was just a dream.' Tears were still falling down her cheeks. 'No,' she said angrily. 'It wasn't *just* anything.' She shook her head slightly, as if trying to shake a memory loose. 'I can't remember much, apart from the fact I couldn't breathe. My lungs were burning, my vision blurred, and I just couldn't breathe. I know it must have been a dream, but I've never dreamt *anything* as vivid as that. I've never felt so close to death before. Not even when...' Her voice trailed off, leaving the sentence unfinished, and I knew enough to leave it alone.

Instead, I wrapped my arms around her, giving her a reassuring hug. 'It's okay,' I said soothingly. 'It's over now.'

'But it's not, is it? Not while we're both in this house. I'm not really sure if I truly believed what you said about a ghost before, not deep down. I thought it would be fun to investigate, to play along. But I was wrong. I need to go and you need to come with me. It's not safe for you either.'

I thought about what I had seen. I wasn't sure if I would ever get the image of her cold lifeless eyes out of my mind. I nodded. 'Okay. Let me just grab some things.'

'No.'

'No?'

'No.' The expression on her face was deadly serious, her face pale with shock. 'Come back for them in the morning once the sun has come up. Let's just get the hell out of here.'

I picked up last night's clothes from the floor, undoing my dressing gown and then slipping on my pants and trousers before pulling a jumper over my head. I checked my trouser pockets; I had my keys, wallet and phone. That was all I really needed.

'Okay. Let's go,' I said, turning to face her, but she had already left.

When I reached the bottom of the stairs, Maddy was standing by the front door, holding my coat in her hand. I slipped my feet into my shoes, not bothering to tie the laces, and followed her out.

It was dark outside and the rain was coming down hard, almost flying horizontally in the strong winds.

'Let's take my car,' I said. It was almost quicker to walk to her house than to drive the slow path through the forest to the main road and back down to her house, but neither of us was in the mood for getting soaked to the skin and frozen.

As I drove the car along the narrow rutted lane between the trees, they seemed more oppressive than normal, leaning in closer. Branches kept swaying down from above or in from the sides, almost as if they were straining to block our path. If you'd asked me at the time, I couldn't have sworn that it was all just the wind. But then, with a final twist around a bend, we were through and onto what passed for the main road. It felt like we had barely travelled any distance along it when I was turning off again, down another long gravel drive to Maddy's house. Thankfully, the path to her house lay next to the forest rather than through it.

I pulled my car up alongside hers and we both ran to the porch, Maddy frantically unlocking the door before we could get too wet. We both tumbled inside.

Sombrely, we took off our wet shoes and coats. There was a clock on the wall, and I could see that it was not quite two in the morning. Maddy had noticed the time too.

'I need to get up for work in the morning,' she moaned in a voice that was barely more than a whisper. 'I don't think I'll be able to sleep much, but I need to try.'

I nodded in agreement and we both crawled our way up the stairs into her bedroom, where we stripped down again and climbed into bed.

'Hold me,' she whispered as we lay in the darkness facing each other. It sounded like she was trying to hold back tears.

I wrapped my arms around her, holding her tight. I was tentative at first; I half feared that her skin would be cold and damp, the lifeless frigid skin of a corpse. I was relieved when it was warm and soft to the touch, cursing myself for even thinking it would be otherwise.

I still hadn't told her what I had seen before we woke, that she hadn't been alone in her nightmare and that this had been some kind of shared vision. I didn't know whether it was meant to be a warning or a premonition, but either way it had scared the hell out of me, and she was scared enough already without adding to her worries.

'Do you think we're safe here?' she whispered.

'I think so,' I whispered back with no real justification. 'I've never seen any evidence of anything outside of the house.'

She gave a tiny nod, almost imperceptible, and I hugged her even tighter.

'So what do we do now?' I asked.

'Well, I think you ought to stay here for a while,' she said. 'I don't want you going back into that house alone.'

'Okay,' I agreed. 'But what do we do about the ghost?'

Maddy thought quietly for a moment. 'We need to see what we can find out about that house's history. I've got some friends at work that should have access to the council's historic records – I'll have a quick chat when I'm on a break tomorrow. Can you do some research online? See what you can find?'

'Sure. I'll see what I can do.'

'You can use my laptop. It's in the office across the hallway. The password... the password is *Michael1982*.' That had been the name of her fiancé. 'It doesn't mean anything,' she added.

'I know. It's fine,' I reassured her.

'If I'm gone when you wake yourself up, make yourself at home. I finish at two and should be back about half an hour later.'

Chapter 10

When I woke in the morning, I made myself a coffee and then set myself the task of finding out as much about the previous owners of Lake View Cottage as I could.

I sat down at Maddy's laptop, logging in with the details she'd given me. I paused momentarily as the computer logged me in and her background wallpaper popped up. It was a picture of her looking a few years younger, sitting with another man, smiling and giggling. It looked like they were at a party, and they looked utterly in love. This must have been Michael, her fiancé.

Her choice of wallpaper had taken me by surprise. There had been no obvious pictures of him around the house that I had seen... but then again, there hadn't been many pictures of anyone, except for the single old photo of her parents.

There was no point being stupid about this, I told myself. They had been engaged and so had obviously been deeply in love. As for our relationship? I didn't really know where I stood. I had strong feelings for Maddy, and she obviously felt something for me, but I still didn't know where this was going. For all I knew, I could just be a fling, a holiday romance for the short time I lived in the cottage.

It had thrown me, but I knew there was no point getting hung up on this. When she was ready to talk to me about Michael, she would. As for us... Well, I supposed only time would tell.

I returned to the task at hand. The Land Registry, the government department responsible for holding details on property ownership, was the obvious place to start, but I was disappointed to see that their details only went back as far as 1994 – not nearly far enough. With some further investigation, I discovered they had a digital archive of old records going back as far as 1862, but it seemed to be impossible to find details of a property by its address. You were only able to search by the owner's surname, which was entirely the wrong way round for my purposes.

I turned to genealogy websites instead, picking the largest one I could find. All it took to access their information was my credit card details. Again, the ability to search through their records was intended for people trying to look up their ancestors by name, but it was still possible to search by a location, if not a specific residence, and for a small village like this there hopefully shouldn't be too many records to search through. I started by looking through their census records, trying to find anyone registered at Lake View Cottage. It was a tedious process, and after half an hour of fruitless searching, I stopped. I sat back and thought for a second. There had to be a better way of doing this.

A quick glance at my watch confirmed what my stomach was trying to tell me; it had gone noon and was time for lunch. I made myself a sandwich and another cup of coffee from what I could find in the kitchen, and then moved to the living room, looking out of the window at the lake as I ate. Then it came to me; maybe I had access to some more direct sources of information. I pulled my mobile from my pocket and dialled my agent.

'Peter!' came Steve's eternally cheerful voice over the phone. 'How's the book going? Is the location inspiring you yet?'

'Fine,' I lied. 'It's progressing well. Look, I've got a favour to ask of you.'

'Sure, go ahead.'

'I was wondering if you could reach out to Ed Steele through your connections. See where he is these days; see if he'd agree to meet with me for a chat?'

'Why? Is there a problem?' His cheerful disposition had changed to concern now.

'Oh no,' I lied again. 'Just thought it would be nice to meet up, one author to another. Professional curiosity, you might call it.'

'Well... okay,' replied Steve. He didn't sound convinced. 'I've got to say, though, I don't know if he's even alive. He hasn't written anything for... oh, at least a couple of decades.'

'If you could see what you can do, I'd be grateful.'

'Okay, I'll do my best. I'll see if he's still got representation, and if so I'll reach out to them, but I wouldn't hold my breath...'

'That's fine. Whatever you can do.'

'Well, okay. I'll leave you to get on with your work and call you back later to let you know how I get on.' And with that, he hung up.

Next, I scrolled back through my dialled numbers until I found the number for the letting agency. I tapped on their number to re-dial them.

'Alpire Letting, How can I help you?' came the voice of the elderly receptionist again.

'Hi, it's Peter Banner again here. I'm renting one of your houses, Lake View Cottage down in Treleven. I was wondering if I could ask you a few questions.'

I could hear some tapping on a keyboard at the other end. 'Is this about the repair work you had done the other day?'

'No. That was all fine, this is... something else.'

'Okay...' said the woman hesitantly. 'How can I help you?'

'I was wondering if you knew anything about the history of the house?'

'The *history*?'

'You know... who owned it previously, whether anything... *interesting*... ever happened there in the past?'

'Interesting?' She didn't seem to understand what I wanted. I can't say I blamed her.

'You know. Newsworthy.' I couldn't bring myself to ask if it had ever been haunted, if anyone had ever been killed there. Despite everything I had been through, it still seemed so ridiculous.

'No, not as far as I know,' she muttered. 'But I'm not too familiar with that property. Hold on a moment.'

I heard the phone being laid on the desk and then the sounds of movement and cabinets being opened in the distance. She returned to the phone a few moments later.

'I've got the records for that property in front of me, but there's nothing out of the ordinary there. It says here that the previous owner had owned it since the seventies, although he hadn't lived there for a long time. Is there anything specific you want to know?'

I sighed. 'No, I suppose not.' Then a thought struck me. 'The door to the attic is locked – do you know what's up there?'

'That'll just be used for storage. Cleaning supplies, tools, that kind of thing. Nothing you need to worry about. It'll be kept locked mainly to keep kids out.'

I sighed again out of frustration, and then realized that she had probably heard this.

'Look,' she said. 'I don't know much about the house myself – I'm just the receptionist here. But I could ask around, find out who dealt with the purchase of the property – they may well have done some research into its history, that kind of thing. I could get them to give you a call.'

'That's great,' I said. 'It's very kind of you.'

With both of those avenues covered, I returned to the laptop and the census data, letting out a low involuntary sigh. It was going to be a long afternoon.

✳ ✳ ✳

After another hour of fruitless searching, I decided I needed a break. Maddy wanted me to stay here with her and I wasn't going to disagree, but I was going to need some fresh clothes and toiletries. It would be better to head back to the cottage and pack a bag while the sun was still up.

As the front door to Lake View Cottage opened before me, I was struck by the cold silence inside.

'Is anyone there?' I called sheepishly as I stepped inside.

I reckoned I should get this done as quickly as I could. I bounded up the stairs two at a time and went first for the bathroom, grabbing my toothbrush and razor. Then I went to my bedroom, pulling a bag down from where I had stuck it on top of a wardrobe. I shoved a few sets of clothing in there – everything I should need for a few days. If I'd forgotten anything... well it wasn't a long trip back here again.

As I stepped back out of the bedroom, I stopped. At the end the landing stood the steep narrow stairs up to the attic. I still didn't know what was actually up there; maybe it was time to find out. Slowly, I crept up the steps, stopping as I grasped the brass doorknob. It turned in my hand, but the door didn't open. It was still locked and I hadn't seen any spare keys anywhere around the house – I suspected the letting agency had them all.

I needed to know, though. What was on the other side of the door? I bent down, getting a better look at the lock. It didn't look strong – like it was designed to stop accidental entry, not keep out determined burglars.

There wasn't a lot of room on the narrow stairs, and I tried bashing against the door with my shoulder. It wobbled but didn't open; I wasn't able to get enough power behind it. Instead, I braced myself against the wall opposite and then raised my leg, kicking the door as hard as I could next to the lock.

There was a loud bang as the wooden frame splintered and the door burst inwards. *There goes my security deposit*, I thought to myself as I stepped inside.

I hadn't known what to expect, but it hadn't been anything quite so underwhelming. The attic was almost empty. On the floor next to the door were a toolbox and several tins of paint. Down the other end of the room, near one of the dormer windows, a white sheet was draped over something square. I walked across the dusty boards, grabbing hold of the cloth and ripping it away. Underneath, there was only a wooden packing case containing a few sheets of wallpaper and some half-used tins of paint.

Disappointed not to find anything of interest, I plodded dejectedly back down the steps and along the landing. As I passed the blue room, I stopped, thinking that I really ought to bring my laptop with me; that way I could always do some more writing if the urge took me, or Maddy and I could both do some online research at the same time. The door to the room stood ajar, and I pushed it open, stepping inside.

As I stepped across the room, I stopped dead. Maddy's watercolour was hanging on the far wall, just where I had left it, but something was very wrong. The colours were smudged, as if water has been running down the picture, smearing the beautiful work that she must have put so much time into. Even from this distance, I could see a discoloration of the wallpaper under the picture where the paints had run down the wall. All that was left of Lake View Cottage was a smudged black mess.

Grabbing my bag tightly by the handles, I turned, running down the stairs, out of the house and back to Maddy's. It wasn't until I had arrived back, panting and gasping for air, that I realized that I had forgotten to grab my laptop. I had only wanted to get the hell out of there.

❋ ❋ ❋

It was just after three when I heard the front door open and Maddy came in.

'Aren't you a bit later than expected?' I said as I checked my watch. 'Is everything okay?'

She nodded. 'I hung around to have a quick chat with some colleagues from another department, to see what I could dig up.'

'And did you discover anything?'

'Well... no,' she said with a sigh. 'Although I did arrange to get access to the central library's main archives if we need to look anything up. They've got all kinds of historic records there which aren't generally available to the public without permission.'

'What kinds of things?'

'Lots of old local newspapers, council records, that kind of thing.'

'Electronic, or paper?' I asked.

'Mainly still microfiche. Some of it's been digitized, but most of that is now publically accessible. What about you?'

'I've been scouring through online records from genealogy websites, looking through census records and the like, trying to find anything. I've only had limited success.'

'*Limited success* meaning...?'

'I've found some names of people who I think may have lived in the cottage before the Steeles.'

'Okay, that's a good start.'

'Yeah, but I don't have much apart from names. There's also a couple of other possible leads. I rang the company I rent the house from, to see if they have any information about previous owners or the history of the house. I'm waiting to hear back from them.'

'Okay.' She didn't sound particularly optimistic.

'I also rang my agent and asked if he could get in touch with Ed Steele, arrange a meeting.'

'Well, that could definitely shed some light on the situation,' said Maddy, the expression on her face brightening. 'If we could talk with him, he'd presumably have a wealth of information. He lived in that house for over a decade; the things he must have seen...'

'Yeah... but my agent didn't seem hopeful. He wasn't even sure if Ed Steele was still alive. He hasn't written anything for the best part of thirty years.'

'So... where does that leave us?'

'Well, I've got a couple of names and dates from the census data. While we wait for my agent and the rental company to call back, we could search through the library records and see if there's anything in local newspapers or records... I reckon that's worth a try. When can we go?'

'I've got tomorrow off work,' said Maddy. 'Fancy a trip to Exeter?'

'Sounds good to me,' I said with a grin.

Maddy nodded and stood up. 'I'll go make the call, check it's okay,' she said as left to go and use the phone.

I stood up myself, stretching my legs and looking out of the window at the landscape beyond. It looked like it was going to rain again.

As I was waiting for Maddy to return, my phone started to vibrate in my pocket and I pulled it out – it was from a mobile number that wasn't in my contacts.

'Hello?' I said.

'Hi there, is this Peter Banner?' It was a man's voice that I didn't recognize.

'Yes?'

'This is Ian Reynolds from Alpire Letting. I believe you rang earlier enquiring about the history of the house you're renting.'

'Yes, that's correct.' All of a sudden I was excited, my nerves tingling.

'I've got to say, it's quite an unusual request.'

'I'm an author,' I started. 'My reason for renting the cottage was to give me a change of surroundings, a change of scenery. I was hoping that maybe the history of the place could give me some inspiration.' I wanted to give a plausible-enough reason for wanting to know the history of the house without sounding too weird. If there was information they wouldn't normally disclose, I wanted him to trust me, to open up to me. 'Sometimes knowing the background of a place – its history, its secrets – that can really help to get the creative juices flowing.'

'Well, I'm sorry to disappoint you, Mr Banner, but I'm afraid I don't really have a lot of information to give you.'

'Oh.' I gave a deflated sigh, my shoulders slumping involuntarily.

'The only history of the house I have is that it had been owned by the same family for almost forty years, although it hadn't been regularly inhabited for about the last thirty. We did all the background checks, surveyors' reports, that kind of thing, and they all came back clean. Although it hadn't been inhabited, the previous owner had had some management company check in every few months and fix up any issues. It wasn't in great condition, but could have been an awful lot worse – we mainly just had to fix some cosmetic issues to get it up to code for renting.'

'Oh,' was all I could manage again. I turned to look out of the window again. Small drops of rain were starting to hit the window.

'So you don't have any issues with the house?'

'No,' I lied. I didn't think he'd quite believe my story. 'It's all fine. As I said, I was just looking for some inspiration.'

'Well, I'm sorry I couldn't be more help.'

When I turned around to face the room again, I saw Maddy in the doorway.

'Anyone interesting?' she asked.

'It was the letting company. It's a dead end, I'm afraid. They don't have any information that would help us. What about you?'
'The library's open from ten 'til three tomorrow. I told them to expect us shortly after ten.'

Chapter 11

We arrived at Exeter library at five past ten, having parked in the local multi-storey car park. There wouldn't be a problem leaving the car there all day if necessary.

When we arrived, Maddy introduced herself to the woman on the front desk, who I was relieved to find was expecting us. She led us through to a dusty back room packed with shelf after shelf, all filled with old cardboard boxes. Once the overhead fluorescent lights had flickered on, she led us to a row of desks set against the back wall of the room, on which were sat a pair of microfiche readers and an old desktop computer. After we were settled, she left us to go and fetch the records we were after – local newspapers and records for the first half of the twentieth century.

She returned a few minutes later carrying a small box containing all the microfiches of local papers. Then she logged in to the computer and showed us the search program that could look for any local records for that time period, although she warned us that there might not be too many. With all the cutbacks, digitizing all the old records hadn't been a priority in the last few years.

The librarian had brought us the local newspapers from 1900 to 1969, and we decided to work through them chronologically, splitting the work between us. Fortunately, there was only one local paper covering Treleven for most of this time period, with a single edition every two weeks until about 1948 – fewer during the wars. Even so, we would have to work fast in order to cover them all in a single day. We'd have to skim through most of them, focusing on main headlines and obituaries.

It was almost noon when we found our first item of interest.

'I may have found something,' muttered Maddy.

'What?' I asked, turning to face her.

'There's an obituary in this paper for a woman dying aged just twenty-three, back in 1922. Her name matches one of the names you found on the census for that time: Elly Irwin.'

'Well, that's certainly a young age to die.'

'The problem is, I've also found a record of an announcement of a birth with the same surname – Bethany Irwin – on the same date.'

I thought for a second. 'You think her death was as a result of child-birth?'

Maddy nodded. 'Not that uncommon back in those days, unfortunately. Especially for home births. What do you think, though?'

I sighed. 'It's a premature death, before her time, certainly, but...'

'It's not exactly the kind of thing you associate with a haunting,' she agreed.

'Not unless it was a murder *disguised* as a death during childbirth?' I suggested

'You think the husband waited for her to give birth and then killed her, making it look like a complication?'

'That certainly would be cold-blooded,' I said. 'The kind of thing you might want to hang around and extract revenge for.'

'It's possible...' she said with a shrug, '... but it feels unlikely. We should keep looking for now, see if there's anything else related to her or her death – something like a police investigation.'

We continued searching, but couldn't find anything else related to Elly Irwin. If her death truly was foul play, then no one at the time seemed to have suspected anything – at least as far as the local news was concerned.

We worked our way through lunch, eating some snacks that we had brought with us. By the time I finally found something of interest, it was nearing two o'clock.

'Come and have a look at this,' I called to Maddy.

'What is it?' she said, shuffling her chair over to look at my screen.

'This is from 1952,' I said. 'It's a report about a young woman called

Harriett Ledbrook being pronounced legally dead. She had been missing for ten years; just disappeared one day and was never seen again.'

'And she lived at Lake View Cottage?'

'According to the census, yes,' I confirmed. 'In 1939.'

'So what happened?' asked Maddy.

'She was a teenage girl when she disappeared – last seen outside near the lake. Everyone assumed that she had drowned, although after an extensive search no body was ever found. No one could ever disprove that she hadn't just run away, though.'

'She would have disappeared in 1942. It would have been during the war.'

'Yes,' I agreed. 'Who knows what could have happened.'

'And someone going missing, presumed dead, but the body never found. That *does* sound like something from a ghost story.'

'Yes,' I agreed again. 'Maybe she was murdered, her body hidden away, the true killer never found.'

'Makes me shiver just thinking about it,' said Maddy. 'Do you think Harriett is our ghost?'

'It's our best guess so far,' I said. I looked at my watch. 'We've still got sixty minutes until the library closes. Let's see if we can find anything else.'

We rushed through the remaining records for the next hour, just managing to get through the last of the papers before the librarian returned to tell us the library was closing. We hadn't found any other leads, and Harriett Ledbrook was still looking like our best chance, although we still had no direct evidence linking her to the haunting.

Maddy was driving us home and we were drawing near when a call came through to me from my agent. I frantically accepted the call.

'Steve!' I called enthusiastically. 'Any news?'

'Well,' he said slowly. 'There's good news and bad news.'

'What's the good news?'

'Ed Steele is still alive, even if he isn't writing any more. In fact, he lives near a village called Bishop's Cross, not a million miles away from where you are now.'

'Okay... and the bad news? I think I can guess.'

'He doesn't want to talk to you. Doesn't want to see anyone, in fact, *especially* anyone to do with writing or publishing. He's turned his back on the whole thing. Hasn't done a single interview since the publication of his last book back at the end of the eighties. I bet his agent must love him – the proverbial cash cow for almost a decade and then he just stopped dead.'

'Well, thanks for trying, anyway,' I said. 'I owe you.'

'Hey, just keep publishing the novels and we'll call it quits,' said Steve.

I still didn't have the heart to tell him that I'd barely started the next one, despite all his encouragement. I said my goodbyes and hung up the phone.

'So no luck on Ed Steele then?' said Maddy. She had obviously heard enough of the conversation to get the gist of it.

'No. He doesn't want to talk to me or anyone else.'

'Another dead end then.'

'*Maybe*,' I said with a shrug. 'He still lives not too far away from here – near somewhere called Bishop's Cross. Do you know it?'

She nodded. 'It's another small village, about half an hour from here. What are you thinking?'

'He may not want to talk to me, but I still want to talk to him. It's a small village... how hard could it be to find him?'

'These small villages can be quite insular, quite private. It might be harder than you think.' She pulled off the main road into her driveway, pulling up next to my car, which was still parked outside her house. 'When are you thinking of going?'

I looked at my watch. It was half-past three. 'I've still got an hour or two of daylight left. I'll head off right now and see what I can find.'

'What about me? I'm coming too.'

I shrugged. 'Why not. Let's take my car, though, give you a break from driving.'

Half an hour later, I'd parked my car in a space on the high street of Bishop's Cross – or what passed for a high street, anyway. It was little more than a small collection of run-down shops and a village pub – *The Plough and Harrow.*

We climbed out of the car, shivering in the cold wind, and looked around. 'What now?' asked Maddy. The light was already starting to drop.

'I don't know,' I said, looking up and down the street. I had no real plan, but as I scanned the shops, an idea struck me. 'I've a quick errand to run first,' I muttered. I skipped across the street, with Maddy following close behind me. My destination was one of the local shops: a small book-store.

A bell rang over the doorway as I stepped inside, an old man looking up from behind the counter as if woken by the high-pitched jingle. I couldn't imagine that trade was brisk in there at the best of times, let alone on a cold dark evening like today.

'I'm afraid we're closing in just a few minutes,' he said with a cough.

'That's okay,' I replied. 'I know what I want. I'll just be a moment.'

'What are you after?' asked Maddy, but I just gestured for her to follow me.

The shop was cramped, with narrow corridors squeezed between floor-to-ceiling bookshelves. I headed for the fiction section and started scouring the shelves, kneeling down at the collection of books I was after. When I stood up again, I was holding a thick hardback novel; I opened the back cover, looked inside and then closed it again. 'This will do,' I said with an air of satisfaction.

'What is it?' asked Maddy.

I showed her the book: *The Haunting of Lady Jane* by Ed Steele. Then I opened the back cover. On the inside of the dust cover was a picture of the author. 'It may be old,' I said quietly, not wanting the shopkeeper to over-hear, 'but it's the best we've got to try and identify him.'

Maddy nodded, and I took the book over to the counter to pay for it, handing over a twenty-pound note and not receiving much back in change. When he didn't mention anything about Ed Steele living in the village, I thought I'd try my luck.

'Is he a local author?' I asked.

The shopkeeper looked at me quizzically over his glasses. 'Can't say I'm aware of that.'

'I heard he lives around these parts. He doesn't do any book signings? I wouldn't mind making this a signed copy. I might even be willing to pay for a signed inscription,' I added, hoping that might tempt him.

'Does this look like a shop where authors might carry out book signings?' he asked rhetorically. I had to admit it didn't. It looked like barely anyone had visited in months.

'But he does live near here?' I pressed.

The shopkeeper shrugged. 'Maybe, maybe not. Can't say I know to be certain. I do know he hasn't written for quite some time though... at least as far as I'm aware.'

'But you still carry his books.'

He shrugged again. 'They're still reasonably popular, despite the years.'

If he did know anything, he obviously wasn't going to bite. 'Okay,' I said cheerily. 'Thanks for the book.'

'Have you ever read any of his books?' asked Maddy once we were outside again.

'Me? I don't think so,' I replied. 'If I did, it would have been back in the late eighties or nineties. I would only have been a toddler when his first book came out, barely in secondary school when he stopped. What about you?'

She shook her head. 'Like I said before, I'm not really into that kind of fiction.'

I nodded. 'I remember you saying that when I asked if you'd read *my* books.'

'I have bought one of yours, though,' she said.

I hoped the expression on my face reflected surprise. 'What do you think?'

She shrugged. 'I haven't finished it yet. I've been too busy at bedtime,' she said with a wink. 'But I suppose it's okay if you like that kind of thing,' she added.

She obviously didn't feel the need to try and spare my feelings. I hoped that was a good sign for our relationship. It felt good that she could be open and honest with me, and not with the bitterness and scorn that my ex-wife still held for me.

'So what now?' she asked as we stood shivering in the street. 'We know what he looked like thirty years ago, but to be honest, I'm sure we could have got a similar photo from Wikipedia.'

'Now,' I said, 'we go to the font of all small talk and gossip for a small village...'

'The church coffee mornings?'

I shook my head. 'The local tavern.'

✳ ✳ ✳

The Plough and Harrow was quiet and gloomily lit – although to be fair, it was only four thirty on a Thursday afternoon. A couple of fruit machines sat flashing silently in one corner, a collection of old concert posters on the wall next to them. At the back of the bar, another small area housed a pool table. We were the only patrons in there.

I stepped up to the bar, Ed Steele's book under my arm.

'What can I get you?' asked the man behind the bar. He was a plump middle-aged man with a bushy brown beard and a ruddy complexion.

'I'll have a coke,' I said. I turned to Maddy.

'I'll have a white wine,' she said, and then when she saw my expression added, 'What? I'm not driving.'

'Ice and a slice?' asked the barman.

'What? Oh... yeah,' I replied, and the barman turned around to face the rear of the bar where he starting slicing a lemon.

I took the opportunity to place the book on the bar, and Maddy and I both drew up stools.

'I've heard he's a local man,' I said to the barman once I'd paid for the drinks.

'I'm sorry?' said the barman.

I tapped on the book. 'Ed Steele. I've heard he's local.'

The barman just shrugged. If Ed Steele did live around here, he obviously wasn't much of a local celebrity.

'We're both big fans,' I said, gesturing to Maddy.

'If I could get an autograph, or a signed copy of one of his books, well, that would just be the best thing ever,' she said with overexaggerated glee. I shot her a look to tell her that she was laying it on a bit thick.

The barman sighed, and leaned forwards on the bar, coming closer to us. 'Between you and me, he does live locally,' he said in hushed tones, as if worrying about eavesdroppers. 'But...' he added, when he saw the smiles growing across our faces, 'he's a man who likes his privacy. I haven't seen him for years. He definitely doesn't do book signings, or conventions, or whatever it is they do these days. I wouldn't hold your breath over getting your book signed.'

'So he doesn't come in here?' I asked.

The barman shook his head. 'Like I said, I haven't seen him myself in a long time.'

'You don't know where he lives?' asked Maddy, smiling sweetly.

'Can't say that I do, and even if I did, I'd respect his privacy enough not to give it out to any Tom, Dick or Harry that came asking for it.'

'Well, I can respect that,' I said with a sigh.

'And I don't think you'd find many people around here who'd behave differently,' he added. 'We're quite a tight-knit community.'

'Even if Ed Steele doesn't play much of a part in it.'

'Aye, even so.'

'Well, thanks for your time,' I said, picking up my drink and taking a long sip. The barman turned away, heading off towards a table in order to collect a couple of used glasses.

'So, what now?' asked Maddy once we were alone again.

'I guess we finish our drinks, and then... I don't know.' Maddy didn't know what to suggest either.

We drank our drinks quickly and in silence, and then got up to leave, Maddy leading the way. Dusk had fallen now and the street lights were turning on, giving the road a dull yellow hue. The cold wind was blowing even harder now and I turned up my collar to keep it out.

Several cars were coming down the street towards us as we walked slowly and dejectedly back towards my car. I had paused, waiting for the other vehicles to pass before we crossed the road, when Maddy grabbed my hand.

'Get in your car,' she suddenly yelled. She yanked me by the arm as she started across the road, forcing one of the oncoming cars to slow down.

'What the hell?' I clamoured, apologizing to the driver of the car with a wave of my hand.

She broke away, running round to the passenger side of the car. 'Start the engine!' she barked at me. 'Don't let that car get away!'

'What car?' I shouted back without slowing down. I opened the door, slipping my key into the ignition and starting the engine.

'Go!' she urged.

I could see in my wing mirror that there were cars coming up from behind, but I thought I could make it. I put the car in first, flicked the indicator and floored it, the tyres slipping momentarily for a second, spraying dust and gravel behind the car as I shot out of the space. The car behind beeped its horn and flashed its lights, but more out of annoyance than danger.

'Who am I following?' I queried, once we were moving in the flow of traffic. 'And why?'

'The Jaguar three, no, four cars ahead,' said Maddy. 'I'm not sure if I was just seeing things or not, it was just for a split second, but...'

'What?'

'You'll see when we catch up to him.'

'Do you need me to overtake?' We were on narrow country roads with quite a few oncoming vehicles, and mine wasn't the sportiest of cars.

'Not just yet.' We were approaching a mini roundabout, and the car directly in front of us was indicating to turn left.

'Which way?' I asked.

Maddy was peering out of the front window. 'Straight on, I think. Yes,' she added as we drew close. 'They've gone straight on.'

I crossed over the roundabout, now only two cars between us and our prey. We followed them for a couple of minutes, praying that we wouldn't be separated by traffic lights, before the Jaguar indicated that it was going to make a right turn at an upcoming junction. It pulled over, slowing down and turning into a smaller country lane. Neither of the cars between us followed it.

'All right,' I said. 'Time to see what caught your attention.'

'Not too close,' said Maddy. 'We don't want to draw attention to us, but just get close enough that we can see the back of the car.'

The road was a narrow and winding country lane with no street lights, and I accelerated slowly, gradually closing the gap between us.

'Fuck me,' I muttered under my breath as we drew near.

'I was right,' whispered Maddy.

The car in front of us was an old Jaguar, possibly an XJ6, and maroon in colour. Its number plate was E573ELE: *E. Steele.*

'The odds of that being anyone other than Ed Steele are quite slim,' I had to admit.

Maddy nodded. 'Drop back a bit, give him some distance.'

I did as she suggested, and settled into a cruise about fifty metres behind him. A minute later, the Jaguar indicated and then took a turning to the left, heading into another long straight road. The hedges on the left side of the road were replaced by a tall brick wall and the Jaguar slowed, indicating as he approached a short driveway. I slowed, keeping my distance. This must be Ed Steele's house.

The short drive between the road and the brick wall was only slightly longer than the Jaguar itself, ending in a pair of tall iron gates, which were parting before it. The Jaguar slipped through the opening and the gates gently closed behind it.

'What now?' I asked, pulling to a stop a short distance down the road from the gates.

'I don't know,' said Maddy with a shake of her head.

'I haven't come this far just to give up now,' I said. I put the car back in gear and drove slowly up to the drive, stopping just in front of the gates. From where we sat, I could see a house at the far end of the driveway, the Jaguar now stopped in front of it, its interior light on. Then the bulb went out, and a few moments later one of the lights in the house went on.

I turned my attention to the gates; they looked tall and strong. There was an intercom mounted on the wall next to them, and I turned off the engine, getting out of the car. Maddy opened her door too, climbing out and joining me by the wall.

There was a button to call for attention and I pressed it. As I waited for a response, I glanced around; looking up, I could see a security camera looking directly at us from atop the wall.

'I guess he used to need to keep out unwanted guests,' said Maddy. 'I'd be surprised if he gets much attention these days.'

No one had replied to the intercom and I pressed the button again. When thirty seconds had passed without reply, I was about to press it again when a crackly voice sounded through a speaker.

'Yes?' was all it said. It was an elderly male voice.

'Mr Steele?' I asked nervously.

'Who is this?' it asked, ignoring my question.

'My name is Peter Banner. I was wondering if I could have a moment or two of your time.'

'I'm sorry—' he began when I cut him off.

'Mr Steele. It's important that I speak to you. I'm currently living in your old house, Lake View Cottage, and—'

'I have no interest in discussing anything with you, Mr Banner. Please leave.'

I turned to Maddy. 'Any ideas?' She just shrugged.

With a crackle, the voice came through the intercom again. 'I've asked you to leave. If you don't go in the next thirty seconds, I'll call the police,' it added.

I didn't know what to do. I sighed. 'Come on, Maddy, let's go.'

The car journey home was quiet and sullen, our mood decidedly dampened. We had both hoped to finally get answers to some of our questions from Ed Steele, but he had quite clearly shown that he wasn't willing to give us anything.

We didn't discuss it as we drove home and made dinner, but as we sat on the sofa drinking a bottle of wine, Maddy was the first to raise the issue again.

'So now that we've drawn a blank with Ed Steele, what do we do now?' she asked.

'I don't know,' I lied. In reality, I had a plan, but it wasn't one I was willing to share with her just yet. I was determined to get the truth out of Ed Steele and I had already made my mind up. I was going to go back to his house and make him talk to me, force a confrontation if I had to. I didn't want Maddy there with me in case things got nasty or he ended up calling the police. I didn't want her to get caught up in anything like that. 'I guess we'll just have to think of something else. I'll probably see if I can find anything more online.'

'I've got work again in the morning,' she said. 'Until around two. But then we've got the weekend together.'

'I've got Lisa for the weekend,' I said, almost apologetically.

Maddy smiled back at me gracefully, 'If you need to go somewhere else to spend time with her, that's fine – I understand completely – but...'

'Yes?'

'If you want to, she's welcome here – you both are. I've got enough bedrooms, and I'd love to get to know her.'

I shuffled closer to her on the sofa, and leant in, giving her a quick peck on the cheek. 'I think she'd like that,' I said, and she smiled back at me. I was a weight off my shoulders not to have to worry about Lisa spending any more time at Lake View Cottage.

'Can I ask you something?' I asked. 'Something personal?'

'You can ask,' she said, 'but I reserve the right not to answer.'

'Fair enough,' I said. 'I was wondering... about Michael. What happened between you two to break off the marriage?'

Maddy sighed, and the expression on her face soured slightly. I thought I could almost see a tear welling up in one eye.

'I'm sorry,' I said, 'I didn't mean to–'

'–No, it's fine,' she said, and I could sense that she was trying to fight back her tears and failing. 'It was a long time ago.'

'I didn't mean to pry,' I said quickly. 'If it's too painful...'

She shook her head, and wiped away a tear from the corner of her eye. 'I'll tell you,' she said, 'but can we then not talk about it again?'

I nodded.

'Michael and I were very much in love, and were engaged to be married.' She paused for a moment to collect her breath before continuing. 'Then, about two months before the wedding, there was an accident. We were driving home late one night in a storm. He was driving too fast, and we came off the road as we went around a corner in the wet. We ended up hitting a tree sideways, and one of the branches came in through the window, hitting him in the head. He died instantly.'

'My god, were you okay?'

She nodded. Several tears were now trickling down her cheeks. 'I don't remember much of what happened. I do remember the police telling me I was lucky to be alive. It could so easily have been me instead of – or as well as – him that died that night.'

'I'm so sorry,' was all I could think of to say, reaching out and wrapping my arms around her. I held her tight and kissed her gently on the forehead. We stayed like that for a little while, the two of us caught in a tight embrace, our heads resting on each other's shoulders.

Maddy was the one who eventually pulled away, but only slightly. She rested her forehead against mine, and I could feel her breath on my face. 'Don't ever leave me,' she whispered.

'I won't,' I replied softly, and as the words left my lips, I realized that I truly meant it.

Chapter 12

I got up with Maddy in the morning, and saw her off on her commute to work. Once she was gone, I prepared myself a travel mug of coffee and then picked up Ed Steele's book. It was a good thick hardback – just as well, as I might have some time to kill.

On the drive back to his house, I took the opportunity to mull over my options. I didn't think ringing the bell and asking to speak to him again would work any better than it had the previous night. The walls around his house were high, but probably not impenetrable; however, breaking in would be even less likely to get him to talk, and I'd probably just end up in a police cell. I decided the best approach would be to wait for him to come out, and then follow him. If I confronted him in person, I thought it would be easier to put my case across. I could appeal to our mutual profession and our shared residency, and hopefully he could see that I wasn't dangerous or crazy. Something had presumably spooked him in the past – something more than just the ghost in the house – something that had turned him into the paranoid shut-in he now appeared to be. When you become a multi-million-selling author of horror novels, who knows what kind of crazy fans must have come out of the woodwork. It was still a problem I'd like to have, though.

With my plan in mind, I parked up in a lay-by a few hundred feet down from his house, the gates just visible before the curve of the road would hide them away. Settling down and making myself comfortable, I got out my coffee and his book. I braced myself for a long morning and started on the novel, glancing up from the page every so often to check that no one was coming or going.

It was almost eleven o'clock – almost two hours into my watch – when I noticed the gates slowly begin to open. I put the book down – I was several chapters through by now – and started the engine. Sure enough, the same maroon Jaguar slipped out through the gap, turning left and heading away from me. I checked my mirrors and then pulled out, following him at a distance. I didn't know if he had noticed my car following him last night, but I didn't want to make my presence too obvious.

His journey didn't take long. After just ten minutes through the winding country roads, he turned off into a car park that was signposted as belonging to a reservoir. I carried on past before turning around and coming back, giving him a minute or so before I pulled in after him, trying not to make it obvious that he was being followed.

As I drew up in a small gravel car park, I could see him walking away from his car with a small dog – a Jack Russell, I thought – pulling him along by his lead. His reason for heading to the reservoir was now clear – it was somewhere to walk his dog.

I parked a few spaces down from him and then climbed out of the car, strolling quickly after him. He had paused momentarily to let the dog off his leash and I took the opportunity to catch up with him.

'Mr Steele?' I called out nervously, just as he was about to set off again.

He turned around, staring curiously at me. 'Yes?' he said. 'Do I know you?'

I could see now that the years had not been kind to Ed Steele. From what I had heard about him, I guessed that he must be at least in his sixties by now, but he looked older – what little hair he had was thin and wispy, his frame wiry. There was a haunted look to his eyes, and he looked cautious at my presence.

'No,' I said, 'but you could say I know you.' I held up the hardback book clumsily. 'I'm a big fan of your work.'

The look of caution on his face turned to one of annoyance. 'I'm sorry,' he said with a bitter snarl. 'That was a long time ago. I don't like to talk about my work any longer.' He turned his back on me and started to walk away from me.

'Please, Mr Steele,' I pleaded. 'This is important.'

He continued to walk away and I started after him. 'I'm living in your old house, Mr Steele – Lake View Cottage – and... I'd like to talk to you about the time you spent there.'

'I'm not interested,' he muttered, continuing to walk away and trying his best to ignore me.

'You can't ignore me forever,' I said, realizing that it made me sound like a stalker only after the words had come out of my mouth. 'We need to talk.'

But he did ignore me, continuing to walk away slowly – although it was probably as fast as he could muster.

I sighed. At this stage, I might as well lay my cards on the table. 'I know your secret, Mr Steele,' I called after him.

This seemed to get his attention. He stopped, although he still didn't turn around. 'You don't know shit,' he snarled, and then started to walk again.

'I know the secret about your books,' I called.

He paused again. 'I don't know what it is you think you know...'

I wondered that myself. How should I tell him that I knew he had lived in a haunted house, that his books were inspired by a real ghost, a ghost that had chased me out of that house in fear of my own life.

'I know the real story behind your novels,' I said. 'I know what happened in that house...'

Ed Steele finally turned to face me. 'I don't know what you think you know, but I don't want to hear another word of it,' he sneered, pulling a mobile phone from his trouser pocket with shaking hands. 'If you don't leave this instant, I'm going to call the police and tell them that you're stalking and harassing me. Straight after that, I'm going to call my lawyer for a restraining order.'

I stopped, taking a step backwards and holding up my hands. 'I'm sorry, Mr Steele. It wasn't my intention to offend you.' This wasn't going the way I had planned.

'Good. Then go away. I don't want to see your face ever again. And if you even think about telling anyone about your stupid fantasies, I'll sue you for slander so fast it'll make your head spin.' His words were angry and bitter, but the expression on his face... he looked scared of me, frightened.

I hadn't expected this. It looked like the phone was shaking in his hand, although I couldn't tell if that was fear, the cold or just his age. I'd come out here angry and ready for an argument... but now I just felt sorry for him. The guy in front of me was a nervous old man, frightened by the stranger who was harassing him while he tried to walk his dog. I'd already wondered if he might have had his fair share of stalkers or intimidation in the past... and maybe I'd dredged all that up again.

I'd been terrified from just a few nights in that house; he'd lived there for nearly a decade. Maybe he had put all that behind him, only for me to bring it all back.

'I'm... I'm sorry,' I said with my head bowed. 'I didn't mean to offend you. I'll go now.'

I turned and walked back to my car like a dog with its tail between its legs. When I reached the car park, I paused and looked back over my shoulder. Ed Steele had continued along the path and was heading away from me, taking his dog out alongside the reservoir, looking for all the world like a beaten man.

✳ ✳ ✳

'What do you remember of Ed Steele from when you were young?' I asked Maddy over dinner that evening.

'I don't really remember anything. I was only five or six when he and his wife moved out, remember?'

'Nothing at all?'

She shrugged. 'I have a vague memory of seeing both of them walking to church on a Sunday morning,' she said. 'I think...' she started, her voice trailing off again.

'What?'

'I think I remember them coming to a birthday party when I was young, giving me a present. I think it's the only memory I have of actually meeting them.'

'What is it?' I asked. She still had a puzzled look on her face.

'Hold on a moment,' she said. She took a final bite of her food, and then put down her knife and fork, wiping the corner of her mouth with a napkin before standing up. 'I'll be back in a moment.'

While she was gone, I took the opportunity to clear my plate and top up both of our wine glasses. I took them into the hallway where I met her coming down the stairs carrying a large cardboard box.

'What's in there?' I asked, but she just smiled and headed for the living room. I followed, putting her wine glass down on the table next to the sofa.

'Now,' she said slowly. 'You have to understand that I don't normally show these to many people, especially after only knowing them for a week or two.'

Now I was really intrigued.

'You have to promise not to laugh,' she added.

'Scout's honour!' I laughed.

'I'm serious,' she replied, a stern expression on her face.

'Okay,' I said, more solemnly this time. 'I promise not to laugh.'

'These are my childhood photos. That's to say, these are some photos of me when I was a child. Mainly me, anyway. There are some of my parents, other children at my birthday parties, that kind of thing.'

'You're thinking... what?'

'I haven't looked through these for a long, long time. But remember when I said that I remembered the Steeles bringing me a birthday present? I think I remember that because there was a photograph of it.'

'One in here?' I said, gesturing to the cardboard box.

She nodded. She reached inside, pulling out a handful of cardboard wallets, each containing a set of old photographs and negatives. She passed me several of them. 'Shall we see what we can find?'

I took the bundle of wallets, placing them on my lap. Then I picked up the one on top, opening it and removing the photographs. This set was of a young girl, which I guessed was Maddy when she was about three or four. It looked like a camping holiday, with pictures of Maddy playing in fields and around tents. Occasionally, she was joined by an older woman who I took to be her mother. In a final picture, they were joined by a bearded gentleman, the three of them standing in front of an open tent.

'Your parents?' I asked, showing her the photo.

She nodded. 'You won't get many of my dad. He was always the one behind the camera.'

'Honestly,' I said. 'There's nothing to laugh at – you look fine. Pretty. You should see pictures of *me* at the same age.'

She smiled back at me. 'Thanks,' she said sweetly.

I opened the next wallet of photos. 'Although...' I said teasingly. 'Here's one of you naked!' The photograph was of her playing in the bath as a young infant, her mother leaning over the side to wash her.

'Stop it,' she chuckled, although I could see her blushing.

'Maybe I could give you a bath later?' I said cheesily.

'Maybe...' she replied coyly. 'I've been a dirty...' then exploded in a fit of giggles. 'I'm sorry,' she said between laughs, as I joined her. 'I've never been any good with any of that kind of thing.'

When the laughter subsided, we returned to the photographs, and a few minutes later our perseverance was rewarded.

'Here it is,' she said, handing me a photograph from the pile in her hands.

The black and white picture was of a woman bending over to give the young Maddy a present. They were standing in what looked like the back garden of her house, and next to the woman was a man that I recognized as Ed Steele. He looked much more like the image on the dust cover of his book than the old man I had harassed earlier that day.

'This is the only one?' I asked.

'I think so,' she said, flicking through the rest of the photos in the pile. 'Yes,' she confirmed when she got to the end. 'As I said, I rarely saw either of them. I don't think they ever went out much, except to go to church on a Sunday.'

'Can you remember what they gave you?'

'I *think* it was a dress. I can't be sure though.'

Something Maddy had said was nagging at the back of my mind, but I couldn't think what it was. Then it struck me. 'Church!' I called out.

'What?'

'When I first came here, I bumped into the vicar at the local church. He also told me that the Steeles left the area after some kind of incident. Couldn't say what it was though. Do you know?'

Maddy shook her head. 'No. I don't think he was the vicar back in those days,' she said. 'He's been here quite a while, but I'm fairly sure he arrived more recently than that.'

'Do you know who *was* the vicar back when the Steeles were around?'

She thought for a moment. 'No. I have some vague images in my mind, but not really. Why?'

'You said that they rarely went out except to go to church. The previous vicar was presumably one of the few people who might have talked to them regularly. Maybe he knows what the incident was that caused them to leave.'

'You think it was something related to the ghost?'

'It could be,' I agreed. 'But if we don't know who he was...'

'The current vicar might know,' said Maddy. 'If he doesn't, then I'm sure he could find out.'

I looked at my watch. It was close to six o'clock. Before I could say anything, Maddy stood up. 'Let's go talk to him,' she said. She was already way ahead of me.

When we parked in the church car park five minutes later, the churchyard was quiet and deserted, although we could see several lights on in the church.

Maddy glanced at her watch, thinking for a moment. 'I think there's an evening service at half-past six,' she said. 'They're probably just getting ready.'

We both hurried in through the front door. Sure enough, we could see the vicar standing at the far end of the church, talking to an elderly woman and handing her some sheets of paper. A couple of other gentlemen were walking along the pews laying out hymn books. We waited until the vicar had finished his conversation before we approached.

He turned to greet us as we neared. 'Miss Wright,' he exclaimed, with a smile on his face. 'And Mr... Banner, was it? Have you come to join our service?'

'I'm afraid not,' said Maddy with a sad smile. 'We actually just wanted to ask you a quick question, if we could.'

'Why, of course,' said the vicar. 'How can I help?'

'If you remember, we were talking the other day about when Ed Steele used to live in this parish, about when he left,' I said. 'I know you weren't the vicar back then, but I don't suppose you remember who was, do you?'

'This would have been the late eighties, yes?' he asked.

I nodded. '1988, I think, or thereabouts.'

He rubbed his chin slowly as he thought for a moment. 'I'm fairly certain that that would have been my immediate predecessor, Reverend Bryce. I've been here since just before the millennium, and I'm fairly certain that when I took over, he had been the vicar for this parish for just over fifteen years.'

'And do you know where we could find him now?' asked Maddy excitedly.

'I can't be certain, but I'm fairly sure he's now the vicar in Buckford. In St Andrew's church there, to be exact.'

'That's great,' said Maddy.

'Thanks very much,' I added, shaking him excitedly by the hand.

'Can I expect to see you at this Sunday's service?' he called out to us, but we were already halfway down the aisle.

'Do you remember Reverend Bryce?' I asked Maddy as we climbed into her car.

'Not really,' she said. 'I couldn't have told you his name, but now that I've heard it... yeah, I think it sounds familiar. When I was a young child, my parents would take me to the church every Sunday morning,' she added by way of explanation. 'As I grew up, not so much.'

'And you know where St Andrew's church is in Buckford?'

'I know where Buckford is. It's a small place. I can't imagine the church will be too hard to find.'

❋ ❋ ❋

Maddy was right. Buckford was another small village, and St Andrew's church was one of its central features. Its tall spire towered over the nearby buildings, illuminated in the dark evening sky by spotlights, like a beacon guiding us towards it.

We arrived at a quarter past seven. Even from the car park, it was obvious that there was a service in progress, the sounds of hymns resonating loudly into the cold night air, and we waited nervously in the car until it had finished. Ten patient minutes later, the front doors of the church opened, and the congregation started to emerge.

Maddy and I waited for the crowd to disperse before we went in through the same main doors.

The entrance led into a small chapel, probably not room for more than a couple of hundred parishioners, even at the best of times. Among the few people that were still milling around, I could see a man picking up hymn sheets from the pews, a slender man who looked to be in his seventies or eighties with thinning grey hair. He was wearing the traditional black shirt and dog collar of a priest.

'Reverend Bryce?' I called out to him.

He straightened up, turning to see who was calling him. 'Yes?' he said. 'Can I help you?'

'We hope so,' I said, and he placed his pile of hymn sheets down on the pew next to him.

'We'd like a quick chat about your time in Treleven,' said Maddy.

'My, that was a long time ago,' said the Reverend. 'What could possibly be of interest from all the way back then?'

'We'd like to talk to you about one of your old parishioners,' said Maddy. 'A neighbour of mine.'

'So did you come to my church in Treleven?' he asked Maddy.

She nodded. 'I don't know if you remember me – Madeleine Wright. I would have been a young girl back then.'

I had brought the old photograph of the Steeles giving Maddy the birthday present at her sixth birthday, and I held it out to him. 'Here, this was Maddy – Madeleine – back then.'

The Reverend took the photograph, peering over the top of his glasses at it. 'Madeleine, you say.'

'That's right. Everyone has always called me Maddy, but you probably knew me as Madeleine. In fact, I think you probably christened me.'

For a moment, it looked as if he didn't remember, but then recognition started to spread across his face. 'Madeline Wright,' he said, nodding to himself. 'And your parents... Chris and... Emily?'

Maddy nodded with a smile, and he returned the favour, handing the photograph back to me.

'Why don't you come through to my office,' he said. 'We can sit and have a chat.'

We followed him up the aisle and through an old door in the corner of the church, into a small cramped office. The walls were lined with shelves, full of old bibles and hymn books.

'Would you like a cup of tea?' he offered, as Maddy and I found a seat and sat down.

'Oh no,' I replied. 'I'd hate to be any bother.'

'So what would you like to know?' he asked as he seated himself behind his desk.

'I was wondering if you remembered anything about a parishioner of yours called Ed Steele,' I asked. 'He was an author, and he lived in Treleven at the time when you were its vicar.'

Reverend Bryce nodded slowly for a moment, as if recalling the memories. 'Yes,' he said a few moments later. 'I think I remember him. He and his wife were regulars at my Sunday morning service.'

'Is there anything you can tell me about him? What he was like?'

'Can I ask why you're interested?' asked the vicar.

'Mainly professional curiosity,' I said. 'I'm also an author, and I've just moved into the same house that he used to live in. Maddy here lived next door to him, as I think I mentioned. Still lives in the same house, in fact.'

'Well, I'm afraid there's not much to tell,' said the vicar. 'He and his wife were very solitary individuals. He wasn't very sociable, kept mainly to himself – never helped out at the church fete or parish council or anything like that. His wife was even more of a recluse – I'm not sure she ever left the house except to come to church on a Sunday morning. I rarely met them other than to speak a few words to them before or after the service.'

'I see,' I said. 'When I spoke to Treleven's current vicar, he said that the Steeles left the village after some kind of incident. I don't suppose you can remember what that was, can you?'

Reverend Bryce sighed. 'Yes, it was a terrible tragedy. His wife, Samantha, drowned in the lake behind their house.'

'She died?' exclaimed Maddy in surprise. She turned to face me, and we exchanged glances.

'Oh yes,' said the Reverend. 'It was a horrible accident. Every morning, Samantha would go for a swim in that lake, and then one day... she just didn't come back. A villager walking her dog saw her swimming earlier that morning, just like she did every day come rain or shine, and when they searched the lake later that day, they found her body floating in the water. The husband was never the same again after that.'

'I... I don't remember that,' said Maddy.

'You were very young,' I said. 'It's possible your parents never told you, to try and shield you from it.'

Maddy nodded solemnly. 'It's the kind of thing they would have done – they were always very overprotective. When I was older, I remember them not allowing me to swim in the lake. That was probably why; they were probably scared the same thing would happen to me.'

A compassionate smile spread across Reverend Bryce's face. 'As for Ed Steele, I don't think he could face living in that house after that, spending every day looking out over the body of water where his wife had died. He left not long after.'

I nodded in agreement. 'The house looks out directly over that lake. Every time he looked out the window, he would have been reminded of it.'

'It was a terrible shame – from the little I saw of her, she seemed like a lovely person – always very kind and humble.'

I sat in silence for a moment. When Harriett Ledbrook had gone missing back in the 1940s, it had always been assumed that she had drowned in the lake, even though the body had never been found. Now a host of questions were running through my mind. Had that actually been the case? Was her death in some way related to Samantha Steele's death? Was her body still lost somewhere at the bottom of a watery grave? Was it the lake that was actually haunted?

'Can you remember when this happened?' I asked, possibly a little too eagerly.

'Let me see,' he said, and he thought for a moment. 'I remember it being an Easter funeral, so it probably occurred around March. I think it may have been 1988. I can't be certain, but I seem to remember the funeral happening not long after we'd finally managed to get the church steeple repaired – it took us almost two years to raise the funds. I'm fairly certain that happened in February 1988, around Valentine's.'

'That would have been around the time of my sixth birthday,' said Maddy. 'Not long after that photograph was taken,' she said, turning to face me and indicating the old photograph in my hand.

I looked again at the photograph, possibly the last photograph taken of Samantha Steele before her death. Something about it was nagging at the back of my mind.

I tried to recall when Ed Steele had released his last book; I was fairly certain it was the very end of the eighties, late 1989 in fact. After my divorce, my own ability to write had been almost obliterated, but for him it must have been so much worse. The grief from losing your loved one in the prime of their life must have been insurmountable. No wonder he had wanted to put it all behind him.

I swallowed. 'I don't suppose you've ever heard any stories about anything odd at the house?'

'*Odd?* What do you mean?'

I shuffled uncomfortably in my chair. 'Stories of anything unusual happening at the house. Odd occurrences. Unexplained phenomenon.' I sighed. 'Any stories of it being haunted.'

Reverend Bryce shook his head slowly, casting a curious glance at me. 'Oh no, nothing like that,' he said cautiously. 'Not that I ever heard of.'

I looked again at the old photo of Ed and Samantha Steele. 'Oh, god,' I murmured. 'I'm sorry!' I suddenly added, realizing I had just blasphemed in front of a vicar in his own church. 'You don't have a magnifying glass, do you?'

'A magnifying glass? I think I might do. My eyesight isn't quite what it used to be.'

He rooted around in one of the desk drawers before removing a small magnifying glass with a metal frame, which he handed to me. I peered through it, closely studying the photograph, in particular Samantha Steele as she bent over to give Maddy her present.

I stood up suddenly, giving both Maddy and Reverent Bryce a start. 'We need to go,' I said to Maddy. Her face was an expression of surprise and worry. 'Thank you very much for your time, Reverend. You've been most helpful.'

I grabbed Maddy by the hand, half pulling her along as I ran out of the church back to her car. 'We need to get to my daughter,' I said. 'Right now.'

✳ ✳ ✳

'Drive,' I barked, as we both clambered into her car. 'Head for the motorway, and don't spare the horses.'

'What's this about?' queried Maddy as she started the engine.

'Just one moment, I promise,' I said. 'I need to speak to Lisa.'

I pulled out my phone with trembling hands and dialled her number. It rang an agonizing number of times before it went through to voicemail. I patiently bit my tongue as I waited for the beep.

'Lisa,' I said as soon as I was being recorded. 'Ring me back the minute you get this – I don't care what time of night it is, just call me back. And... and this is important... if you're wearing the pendant I gave you, take it off. Take it off and put it in a drawer somewhere. I'm coming over right now – I'll explain everything when I see you.'

As soon as I'd hung up, I rang my ex. I didn't particularly want to speak to her, but I needed to know where Lisa was, to know she was alright. When she didn't answer, I hung up and tried the home phone instead. There was no answer there either. I prayed that nothing had happened already. I didn't leave a message – I didn't know what to say in a message to her that I hadn't already left for my daughter. Instead, I turned back to Maddy. 'I could be wrong about this,' I said, 'but I have a terrible feeling about Lisa.'

'What is it?' asked Maddy as she continued to drive. The rain was coming down heavily and she was driving fast, concentrating hard on her driving. 'How's she involved in any of this? And what's this about a pendant?'

'I'll tell you everything,' I said, turning to face her as she sat in the driver's seat. She was hunched forwards, urging the car to go faster. She looked anxious... no, I realized; it was more than that. She looked *scared*. I thought back to what she had told me about her fiancé and how he had died.

She put her left hand out onto the gear stick, contemplating changing down in order to overtake a slower car ahead.

I rested my hand gently on hers. 'Just take it easy,' I said calmly. 'This isn't the best conditions for fast driving.' I didn't want to mention the possibility of having an accident. I wondered how similar tonight was to the night on which Michael had crashed. On that night, they had also been driving too fast on country roads in the rain.

'What about Lisa?' she said, concern in her voice.

'Let me worry about Lisa,' I said. 'You just worry about getting us there safely, okay? We're no good to anyone if we end up in a hedge.' I bit my tongue as I said it, but it didn't seem to have struck a nerve. 'And you can't concentrate fully on the road if I'm explaining my theory to you.'

I lifted my hand from hers, and she returned it to the steering wheel, keeping the car in fifth gear. Her right foot lifted slightly from the accelerator.

'So what is it?' she asked a few moments later. 'This theory of yours?'

'Just hear me out,' I said. 'Tell me if I'm crazy or not.'

'Okay.'

'Back in 1942, Harriett Ledbrook went missing from Lake View Cottage and was presumed to be drowned in the lake, her body never found.'

'Okay.'

'If we assume that's true... well, we know Samantha Steele also drowned in that lake while living at Lake View Cottage. She was presumably a good swimmer; Reverend Bryce said that she swam there every morning. The two can't just be coincidence.'

'Go on.'

'I'm thinking there are one or two possibilities – either Harriett Ledbrook and Samantha Steele were both killed by the ghost...'

'Or else Harriett Ledbrook herself is the ghost,' said Maddy. 'Drowned, her body never found, wandering this earth until her body can be properly laid to rest.'

'And she dragged Samantha Steele down to a watery grave beside her.'

Maddy nodded. 'That sounds more like the plot of a ghost story. But what about Lisa? What about the pendant?'

'About a week ago, Lisa came down to stay for the weekend. It was after you'd first met me, but before anything had really happened. I think I told you that a couple of things really spooked her while she was down. First, she felt like there was a woman in her bedroom in the night, and then she got trapped in the bathroom and swore that there was someone in there with her. We know now it was the ghost, but at the time I just dismissed her fears. Don't I feel like a complete shit right now.'

'Don't beat yourself up,' said Maddy. 'If you hadn't experienced anything yourself yet, then that would be the natural reaction.'

'The thing is,' I said, 'shortly after she arrived, she found a pendant in her bedroom, this small silver thing on a chain. She assumed it was a present from me, and, well...'

'You didn't do anything to change her opinion?'

'No, not really.'

'But where did it come from then?'

'I'm guessing it was from Harriett Ledbrook.'

'And you think Lisa is in danger if she's wearing it? In danger from the ghost? But surely she'd be fine all the way over here.'

'I don't know for certain. I don't know anything for certain any more. But I do know that Samantha Steele was wearing it, shortly before Harriett killed her.'

'What? How do you know *that*?'

The car drew to a halt behind a queue of traffic at a red light, and I reached into my pocket, pulling out the old photograph of the Steeles at

Maddy's birthday party. I tapped Samantha Steele. 'She's wearing it in this photograph,' I said solemnly.

Maddy leaned over, squinting at the photo.

'It's hard to be certain, but when I had a look through Reverent Bryce's magnifying glass... I'd put good money on it being the same pendant – or at least the same design.'

'Shit,' cursed Maddy under her breath, accelerating hard as the lights turned green.

We were about ten minutes away from my ex's when my phone rang in my hands. It was Lisa.

'Are you okay?' I said, almost shouting into the phone.

'What? Of course I am. Why shouldn't I be?' She sounded confused, and I couldn't blame her.

'Okay, okay,' I said, more to myself than to her. 'Where have you been?'

'Just out at the cinema with mum,' she said. 'I've only just turned my phone back on again. What's the matter? What's so important?'

'I can't really explain over the phone. Are you at home?'

'Yeah, I got back just a couple of minutes ago.'

'Okay. We'll be there in about ten minutes.'

'*We?*'

'Me and Maddy.'

There was a momentary pause from Lisa. 'So you two are an item now?'

I looked across at Maddy as she drove through the rain, concentrating hard on the road ahead. 'Yes, I guess we are,' I said, grinning inwardly.

'Does mum know you're coming over?' asked Lisa.

'Err... no,' I muttered.

Lisa sighed. 'It's kind of late for you to be coming over unannounced. I don't know how she'll take it.'

She was right. I hadn't thought about that.

'Especially with another woman,' she added.

I *really* hadn't thought about *that*.

'Look,' said Lisa. 'When you get here, just park up outside. I'll pop out and see you. Mum doesn't need to know you're there.'

'You don't have to cover for me,' I said.

'It's fine. No biggo. You can make it up to me next time you have me.' Well, at least she hadn't written off ever staying with me again after the fiasco of last weekend.

'Okay. I'll text you when I get there.'

'Love you, dad.'

'Love you too.'

We arrived a few minutes later, parking up in the street outside. I send Lisa a quick message telling her we were there, asking her to bring the pendant with her. Then I turned the interior light on in the car, so that she could see us.

Two minutes later, I saw Lisa jogging out of the front door, heading for us with a bag in her hand. She opened the rear door, slipping into the back seat.

'Hi, dad!' she said.

'Hi,' I replied. 'This is Maddy,' I said by way of introduction.

'Nice to meet you,' said Lisa. 'Dad hasn't told me nearly enough about you.'

'I'm sure there will plenty of time to tell you all about me later,' said Maddy with a smile.

'Did you bring the pendant?' I asked anxiously.

She held up the plastic bag. 'In here,' she said, passing it to me. I took the bag from her, peering inside to check it was there before passing it to Maddy. She couldn't help looking inside too, before stuffing it into a cubby hole.

'So what's wrong with it?'

'Huh?

'The pendant. Why's it so dangerous? Is it made out of lead? Poisonous? *Radioactive?*'

'No, nothing like that,' I said.

'Then what's wrong with it?'

'It's kind of a long story,' I said.

'There might be an issue with the original owner wanting it back,' added Maddy.

'The original owner?' said Lisa. 'Is it *stolen?*'

'No, nothing like that,' I said with a shake of my head. 'I'll explain later, I promise,' I added solemnly. 'Just trust me for now. I'll get you another pendant – a better one, I promise.'

'Well, okay, I suppose,' said Lisa. 'Are you still coming tomorrow to pick me up for the weekend?'

I looked at Maddy, who just smiled and shrugged back at me. She'd offered to put up Lisa for the weekend, so we didn't have to stay in Lake View Cottage, but I still wasn't sure just how safe it would be for her... or how awkward.

'It might not be a good idea at the moment,' I said. 'Is that okay?'

Lisa giggled. 'You two love-birds need some alone time?'

I could see Maddy blushing, even by the dim light in the car. 'No, it's not like that,' I said. 'It's... it's complicated. I'm not sure it's safe for you.'

Lisa frowned, not quite understanding, and then shrugged. 'I suppose I can wait another week to see you, especially as I've seen you tonight.'

'Can you tell your mum?'

Lisa nodded. 'She'll probably be pissed if you cancel at the last moment. I'll tell her I've lots of work to do and I'd rather spend the weekend with her. It'll be easier that way.'

'You don't have to cover for me,' I said again. 'You shouldn't have to lie to your mother.'

'It's fine,' she said dismissively. 'And I *do* have lots of work to do. I'll cover for you two this time... but you owe me, okay?'

I smiled at her. 'I'll make it up to you next weekend.' I hoped to god this would all be resolved by then, although I couldn't yet see how.

'We both will,' said Maddy. 'We'll all go out somewhere nice together.'

'I'd like that,' said Lisa. She glanced at her watch. 'I'd better get back before mum wonders where I am.'

'Okay,' I said. 'Stay safe, okay, kiddo?'

Lisa gave me an exasperated look, but then she nodded, a smiled spreading across her lips. 'Will do,' she said, and climbed out of the car, rushing back to the house in the rain.

When she was inside, I turned back to Maddy. 'Thanks for that,' I said.

'I'm just glad she's okay. She seems like a nice kid.'

'She's the best,' I said with a sigh. 'I guess we can go home now. You can take it a bit slower on the way back.'

Lisa turned off the interior light and started the engine again, pulling out into the street. As we rejoined the main roads a few moments later, my phone beeped to tell me I had a text message. I pulled it from my pocket, glancing at the screen.

'It's a message from Lisa,' I said, unlocking the phone.

'Is there a problem?' asked Maddy, suddenly concerned again.

I scanned through the message rapidly, and then smiled. 'Just the opposite. I think you just passed the first test – Lisa says she likes you.'

Chapter 13

It was late in the evening when we arrived back at Maddy's, and we were both tired and weary. Slowly, we both ascended the stairs and climbed into bed.

'Do you mind if we just sleep tonight?' I said. 'I'm exhausted.'

'I was just thinking the same thing,' replied Maddy, giving me a gentle kiss. We both reached for our books; she was now working her way through my second novel, while I was still reading *The Haunting of Lady Jane*.

As I sat next to Maddy, tucked up under the duvet, an odd feeling swept over me as I continued through the book. I had started a new chapter, and there was something about the prose that unsettled me, but I just couldn't put a finger on what was causing it. The words seemed vaguely familiar, but I was sure I'd never read this book before – some kind of literary déjà vu. Maybe it was something about the style, or the language.

I turned to Maddy, resting my hand on her knee and giving it a gentle squeeze. She turned to me, a contented smile on her face.

'Oh fuck,' I suddenly muttered under my breath.

'What is it?' asked Maddy, instantly concerned.

Suddenly I could see it all; I knew what had happened. We had both got it so wrong.

'I need to check on something,' I muttered as I clambered out of bed and started putting my clothes back on.

'What's going on?' said Maddy. She sounded worried.

'I need to check something,' I said. 'Back at Lake View Cottage.'

'You can't be going there *now*?' she asked. 'In the middle of the night?'

'I'll be fine,' I said confidently, although inside I was a little less sure. But this felt right now. I didn't want her to come with me though, just in case my theory wasn't right. I didn't want to put her in any danger.

'You can't be serious?' she pleaded.

'Please just trust me,' I said. 'There's something I need to do. I need you to stay here okay? Just try and get some sleep.'

'Won't you tell me what's going on?'

'I have an idea, but I need to put it to the test,' I said. 'I'm sure I'll be safe – just trust me.'

'Pete...'

'Please.'

She looked at me, studying my face, trying to work out if she could trust me. 'Okay,' she said eventually, 'but hurry back soon.'

I got dressed quickly, pulling a jumper over my head and then slipped my feet into my shoes. 'I'll be back as soon as I can,' I said.

✳ ✳ ✳

The weather had worsened again, the rain as bad as I had seen since I arrived, and I climbed into my car, driving the short distance back to the house and parking out front. I rushed to the front door in the downpour, unlocking it and letting myself in.

Inside, the house was cold and dark. Quiet. I slipped my feet from my wet shoes, leaving them by the door and cautiously stepped into the dining room. I was after my laptop, and had expected to see it sitting on the oak dining table, but it wasn't there. Then I remembered; I had taken it upstairs to the blue room when Maddy had come over for dinner.

I walked up the stairs in the darkness and into the room. My laptop was still sitting where I had left it: on the desk by the window. I stepped over to it and turned it on. By the glow of the screen, I could still see Maddy's water-colour hanging on the wall, the colours streaked and ruined; it gave me the creeps. I picked up the laptop, carrying it back into my own bedroom and placing it on the dresser at the foot of the bed.

I stood over it, muttering to myself as I patiently waited for it to start, and once I had logged in, I opened my word processing software. I started a new document then stood back, watching the flashing cursor, the light of the screen the only illumination in the room. I didn't want to turn any lights on — for once, I wanted the ghost to come.

'Talk to me,' I muttered to the empty house.

I stepped over to the bed and lay down on it. I could still make out the document on the screen; it remained steadfastly blank. I couldn't decide if I was mad or not. I supposed only time would tell.

I lay there in the darkness, listening to the sounds of the storm outside, the hard patter of the rain on the windows. I waited patiently, waiting to see what would happen, but there was nothing. I still felt exhausted, and as I sat in the darkness, listening to the hypnotic beat of the rain on the glass, my eyelids gradually grew heavy, until I slipped into a deep slumber.

I found myself standing on the patio behind Lake View Cottage once more, a cold wind still coming off the lake behind me. I squinted as the low morning sunlight reflected off the windows of the house, and I put my arm up to shield my eyes from the glare.

I felt cold and wet, almost shivering despite the bright sunlight as I walked slowly and hesitantly towards the bay doors. Something was wrong — very wrong. I could feel it in my bones, but still I kept on walking, slowly putting one foot after another until the doors were in my reach.

As I pulled the doors open, I paused momentarily. The room was spotless, meticulously neat and tidy, with not a thing out of place. I stepped inside cautiously. A landscape painting I didn't recognize, not one of Maddy's, was on one wall, and sitting on the dining room table was the same old-fashioned typewriter, still sitting next to a pile of paper.

I turned my head as I caught the sound of running water upstairs. It sounded like someone was running a bath. I felt myself drawn towards it, slowly stepping across the room and then up the staircase. The stairs felt like they would never end, as if I was walking up an escalator that itself was descending.

And then I was there. Standing in front of the bathroom door, although it was now pale green in colour, rather than white.

'Hello?' I called out in a voice that wasn't my own.

I pushed the door open, revealing the dark room inside. The large old-fashioned bath tub stood at the far end of the room, water still pouring from the taps despite the fact that it was almost full.

I hesitantly took a step inside, then another. I stopped next to the sink and turned to face the mirror. It reflected back a face that was not my own, but one I still recognized, frozen in time by a photograph taken almost thirty years ago.

As I stood and stared into the mirror, I saw another face emerge from the darkness behind me. A face filled with hatred and rage.

A loud crash awoke me with a start. My heart was pounding, my breathing rapid. There was sweat on my brow. I knew now, though. I knew I was right.

The storm was still raging outside and I wondered about the crash I'd heard – had it been real, or just part of the dream? Maybe a tree or a branch had come down and broken one of the windows – there were plenty of them standing close enough to the house for that to be possible.

I stood up slowly, stretching my arms and stifling a yawn. A quick glance at my watch told me that I had only been asleep for thirty minutes.

Stepping out onto the landing, I stood in the darkness, listening to the sound of the storm. It was louder now than it had been before, the sound of thunder rumbling nearby with occasional flashes of lightning. There was something about the sound that was wrong, though. It sounded louder downstairs and less muffled, as if a door or window had been left open. A window probably had been broken in the storm, I thought to myself.

Slowly, I descended the stairs. It sounded like the broken window was in the kitchen, and I walked along the hallway, pushing open the door, which stood ajar.

As I suspected, a pane of glass was broken in the back door, and rain was coming in. In a flash of lightning, I could see a puddle on the stone-tiled floor, dotted with shards of broken glass. But something was wrong; there was no tree branch or any sign of what might have smashed the window. In fact, now that I thought about it, I didn't believe that any tree stood near the back door.

There was another flash of lightning, and the creak of a floorboard to my right. I turned and gave an involuntary gasp. Standing in the doorway to the dining room was a figure dressed in black, a thick hood up over his head.

In his hands was a shotgun, and it was pointing directly at me. It looked old, but that didn't stop it being just as deadly.

From a moment, we just stood there in silence, looking at each other. I decided to go first.

'Why did you do it, Ed?' I asked, taking an educated guess at the intruder's identity.

The man in black stood in silence for a moment before pulling his hood down to reveal the withered old face of Ed Steele.

'Break in?' he asked, as if not quite understanding. 'I don't have a key any more. They changed the locks.'

I shook my head. 'Why did you kill her? Why did you kill Samantha?'

He looked back at me, as if studying me intently. 'How did you work it out?' he asked eventually, ignoring my question.

'You wouldn't believe me if I told you,' I chuckled joylessly.

'I suppose it doesn't matter anymore,' he said. 'I just need to know who you've told.'

'Who I've told?'

'Who else knows? Who else knows I killed my wife?'

I thought for a second. If I was the only one who knew, then I was surely a dead man. And I couldn't tell him about Maddy – he'd finish me off, and then head straight over to her house and kill her in her sleep. There was no way I was going to even chance that. I needed another reason for him to keep me alive.

'My agent,' I said in desperation.

'Your *agent*?'

'I'm a writer,' I said. 'Like you. Or like you used to be, anyway. Except you weren't, were you Ed? Was it always Samantha? I'm guessing it was.' I stared him in the eyes, but he just gave a little snort, keeping his gaze directly on me. 'It wasn't grief that stopped you writing after her death, was it?' I continued. 'It was never you in the first place.'

He continued to say nothing, just tightening his grip on the shotgun.

'Then why kill her?' I asked again. 'You were world-famous through her work, rich and successful. Why throw that all away?'

'She was going to leave me,' he replied sourly. 'Once that happened, it would all have dried up anyway. Worse, if she had revealed our secret, then I wouldn't have received any more royalties. It was all coming to an end either way.'

'And no one ever suspected that you weren't the real author?'

'It was a different time back then. No internet, no social media, much easier to live in isolation. Think of all the books published under pseudonyms over the years. The only difference was that even our agent didn't know the truth. Not that it bothered him too much – as long as he received his commission, he was happy to keep accepting the novels. He would have preferred more interviews and publicity – I managed the occasional one – but he didn't want to do anything to disturb the status quo and send us looking for another agent.'

'The truth will come out now, though,' I said, although I didn't feel too confident while looking down the twin barrels of the shotgun.

'Who's your agent?' he asked. 'What have you told him?'

If I couldn't resolve this here and now, I didn't particularly want to drop my agent in it by giving this madman his name. 'I haven't told him anything as such,' I said. 'But he has a draft of my current project,' I added hastily as I saw the shotgun twitch. 'A book about the real history of this house.'

'What have you put in it?'

'Enough. Enough for the truth to come out.'

'Well, if you're taking me down, I'll take you down with me,' he growled, raising the shotgun.

'I can take you to it,' I blurted out. 'I'll take you to my agent's office. We can get the draft back again.' I was winging it now, just saying anything to stay alive. I could worry about the details later. 'It's on a CD. He told me he was planning to look at it next week. That and my laptop hold the only copies.'

Ed looked at me, studying me, trying to decide if I was telling the truth or not.

'Where's your laptop?'

'Upstairs, in the master bedroom.' If he destroyed that, the loss of my current novel would be a small price to pay; no one would mourn its passing.

He nodded. 'Okay,' he said. 'We'll dispose of that first. Let's go.' He'd obviously decided I was telling the truth.

Just then, there was a loud bang from upstairs. It sounded like a door slamming.

He turned towards the sound of the noise. 'Who's that?' he barked. He turned back to face me. 'Who's in here with you?' he snarled.

'No one,' I said. I really hoped it wasn't Maddy, come to join me while I had been asleep. But just maybe it was Samantha – maybe she could help me.

Ed twitched the shotgun, indicating I should head back into the hallway. 'Let's go. Slowly... no funny business.'

I led him slowly back out into the hallway. The lights were still off upstairs, and it was dark and quiet. I stopped a few steps up, unsure.

'Who's there?' called Ed from behind me. 'Come out and show yourself!'

All remained quiet.

I heard Ed take a couple of steps behind me, then he flicked a switch. For a moment, the light at the top of the landing turned on, before there was a loud pop and it went out again, returning the landing to darkness.

'I've been having some problems with the electrics,' I muttered.

There was a sharp prod in my back from the hard barrels of the shotgun. 'Walk,' he said, and I did. The journey up the stairs felt uncannily similar to the same journey in my dream. When I reached the top, I stopped and listened, not quite sure if I could believe my ears. The bathroom door was shut, but there was the undeniable sound of running water from within.

Ed nudged me further along the hallway, towards the bedrooms, so that he could position himself next to the bathroom door. He banged on the door with the butt of the shotgun.

'Who's in there?' he yelled at the door, but again there was no reply. 'Who's in there?' he asked me instead.

'No one,' I replied, turning around to face him. 'I must have left a tap running.'

The look on his face made it clear that he didn't believe me. He gave a brief grunt and then reached for the door handle, grasping it firmly in his left hand while he held the shotgun in his right. He turned the handle and the door opened, swinging inwards.

The sound of running water was louder now – and splashing too.

Ed reached inside with one hand, feeling along the wall until he found the cord for the lights. He gave it a tug and I could hear a click, but the lights stayed off. With a grunt, he reached into his pocket with his left hand and brought out a torch, which he deftly turned on with the press of a button. 'Here,' he called as he threw it to me. 'You go in first where I can see you.' He took a couple of steps back, clearing a passage into the bathroom without ever letting me get too close to him or the gun.

Holding the torch in trembling hands, I walked back towards Ed and then into the bathroom, stopping in the centre. The room was freezing cold and appeared empty, but in the corner, water was pouring from the cold tap into the bath. The bath itself was full, the overflow pipe not quite able to cope, and water was spilling over the edge onto the floor.

'There's no one in here,' I said slowly, the moisture from my breath condensing in the air in front of me.

'Let me see,' said Ed. I could hear him approach, stopping in the doorway. 'Show me,' he said, and I slowly panned the torchlight around the room, stopping on the bathtub.

'Hmm,' he grunted, obviously dissatisfied.

Then something began to happen. Ripples began to form on the surface of the bathwater and more water started to pour over the edge. Something began to rise from the water, an unrecognizable knot of something dark. As it began to lift out of the water, its identity became clear. It was dark black hair, closely followed by a gaunt face and then a torso, a pale rotting corpse emerging upright from the water. The skin was white and putrid, the hair flowing in the air as if caught in unseen eddies of water. It was wearing a tattered black swimming costume and was unmistakably the corpse of Samantha Steele.

Ed Steele stood transfixed in the doorway, frozen in fear as Samantha rose to stand upright in the bathtub. Then she raised one arm to point at him with a bony finger.

There was a deafening bang as Ed let off one of the barrels of the shotgun, and I dived to the floor in an attempt to stay out of harm's way. The shot had ripped into the corpse of Samantha, opening a large cavity in one side of her torso, but she didn't seem to notice. Slowly, she stepped from the bath, her eyes never leaving Ed's. She opened her mouth, an inhuman scream bellowing forth, the bony finger still pointing directly at him. Thick, congealed blood began to slop forth out of her mouth, dripping onto the wet floor at her feet.

It was more than Ed could take. He fired the other barrel, this time going high and wide out of panic, and blowing a large hole in the bathroom wall. Then he turned and ran. He was moving much faster than when I had seen him walking by the reservoir, spurred on by a mortal fear. I half hoped he would fall down the stairs and break his neck.

I took one quick glance at Samantha and then ran after him. I thought his shotgun was the old-fashioned type – only able to hold one cartridge in each barrel. He would be unarmed until he was able to reload it.

He was already halfway down the stairs as I reached the landing. I had stopped at the top of the stairs, unsure whether to follow him or not, when the kitchen light turned on downstairs.

'Are you okay?' came a voice from out of the light. It was Maddy.

She stepped out of the kitchen and into the hallway just as Ed Steele reached the bottom of the stairs, turning to face her. He raised the gun towards her.

'It's not loaded!' I shouted at her, hoping to god that this was true. In his terror, I wasn't sure whether Ed was even aware of this. Sure enough he squeezed the trigger, but the only sound was a quiet click. Maddy took a step forwards, grabbing the gun with both hands, wresting it from his grasp. Then, with a simple swipe she shoved it backwards, slamming the butt of the gun into his head. He crumpled to the floor like an old rag doll.

'Are you okay?' she called out again, this time looking up at me.

'I'm fine,' I replied, bounding down the stairs towards her. She had dropped the shotgun on the floor and we stepped towards each other, grabbing each other in a warm embrace.

'I started to get worried when you didn't come back,' she said. 'I decided to come over despite what you'd said, and then when I was standing outside I heard what sounded like a gun-shot. The back door was open, and... well, you know the rest.' She looked down at the body on the floor. 'Was that *Ed Steele*?'

I nodded. 'He killed his wife Samantha all those years ago,' I said. 'I think he drowned her in the bath, and then dumped her body in the lake to make it look like an accident.' I bent down and checked his pulse. He was still alive, but out cold.

'Then she was the ghost?' asked Maddy.

'Yes,' I said. I stepped into the kitchen, opening a drawer, which I knew contained a length of rope. I rolled Ed Steele onto his back and used the rope to secure his hands behind his back. 'That's not all. Ed never wrote any of his books.'

'*What*?'

'It was Samantha. She was the real author all along.'

'Then that's why he stopped writing after her death. It was never anything to do with grief.'

'No. I'm guessing the one book he released after her death was already mostly – if not completely – finished before she died.' I stood up again, and looked up at the landing. The ghost of Samantha Steel was standing in the shadows looking down at me. She raised one hand out towards me, then slowly bent the index finger inwards, beckoning me towards her.

'Call the police,' I said. 'And an ambulance. I'll be right back.' With a lump in my throat, I slowly ascended the steps once more, towards the waiting shadow. As I crested the stairs and stood on the landing, I could see her slowly walking away from me along the corridor. In the torchlight, I could see wet footsteps behind her which dried out moments later.

She stopped outside the bedroom I had called the blue room and looked at me over her shoulder with cold forlorn eyes before turning and stepping inside.

From the doorway, I watched her step to the far corner of the room. With one finger, she pointed down towards the floor.

'What is it?' I asked.

She mouthed something wordlessly to me, but I couldn't make it out. Then she simply disappeared, transformed into a mass of water, which dropped to the floor, exploding with a splash before slowly dissipating until all that was left was a small dark puddle on the carpet.

'What happened?' came a voice from beside me. It was Maddy. 'The police and ambulance will be here as soon as they can.'

'I'm not sure,' I said. I tried turning the light on, but nothing happened. I guess the circuit breaker for all the upstairs lights had tripped. I shone the torchlight over to the corner where the ghost had stood, and crept cautiously towards it, looking down at the dark stain on the carpet. 'Come give me a hand,' I called to Maddy.

Together, we shifted some of the furniture, and I rolled back the carpet to reveal the floorboards underneath. The stain had bled through the carpet, marking one of the floorboards with its own dark wet stain. I inspected it closely with the torchlight, slowly coming to the realization that, unlike the other floorboards, this one wasn't nailed down. I passed Maddy the torch, and got down on my hands and knees, trying to get a grip on it, pulling at the loose board. I was rewarded on my second attempt, the short piece of wood coming up in my hands.

I gestured for Maddy to pass me the torch again, and she did. I leaned down low over the hole, reaching inside and searching the dark space beneath the floor.

'Is there anything there?' whispered Maddy.

I nodded back to her, and when I removed my hand I was holding a shallow A4-sized cardboard box. Excitedly, I placed it on the floor between us, removing the lid with trembling hands.

Inside, there were hundreds of sheets of yellowing paper, each typewritten with the occasional handwritten correction. On the first page was the title: *My Story by Samantha Steele.*

I flicked through the sheets. Page after page about her; her life story and the life she was forced to live with her husband. All written in secret, without his knowledge.

'We were wrong all along,' said Maddy. 'At least until you guessed the truth. How did you work it out?'

'When I was reading Ed Steele's book, one of the chapters seemed eerily familiar. I was sure I hadn't read the book before, but there was something about the words used, the style of writing... then I remembered. One night, I had stayed up late writing, and had drunk far too much. In the morning when I read back what I had written – what I thought I had written – I found that the story of my two main characters had taken a decidedly dark turn. I put it down to the alcohol and the deteriorating relationship with my ex, but it was her: Samantha. The words weren't the same, but the style of it all... it had undoubtedly been written by the same author. She was trying to tell me her story.'

'She never wanted to hurt us,' said Maddy quietly.

I nodded back. 'She was only ever trying to tell us what had happened to her. Even the pendant... that was probably just intended as a present for Lisa. A present for the daughter she had never had.'

'Ed Steele may have killed her,' said Maddy, 'but she was determined not to let him get away with it, no matter how long it took.'

I nodded to her in the torchlight. 'Hopefully, she can rest in peace now.'

Epilogue

It was a fine autumn morning as Maddy and I walked hand in hand down the high street. The sun was out, the sky was blue, and it was already looking like it would be a hot day.

We slowed and then stopped as we reached a book shop, turning to look through the window at the large pile of hardback books that were stacked on display. Across the cover of each was a stylized picture of Lake View Cottage and in a large bold font was the text: *My Story, by Samantha Steele*. At the bottom of the cover, in much smaller text, were the words: *With an introduction by Peter Banner.*

'Your agent can't be happy,' said Maddy with a smile. 'You never wrote him that novel you promised him.'

I nodded and gave a small shrug. 'And neither of us will get anything from Samantha's story. All parties involved agreed that all the money should go to charity, to help women like her in abusive relationships. Technically, since her death, any royalties that would have been paid to her would go to her husband, and I don't think that's what she would have wanted.'

'So all that potential inspiration for you, and nothing to show for it.'

'Oh, I don't know...'

'What do you mean?' she asked, one eyebrow raised quizzically.

'I'm thinking of writing a book about our experiences.'

She thought for a second, and then turned to face me, stepping up close. 'Will I be in it?' she asked softly, flashing me a cheeky grin.

'Of course,' I said, placing my hands around her waist. 'It's your story as much as mine. If you don't mind, that is?'

She smiled and gave me a brief kiss. 'Of course not. What will you call it?'

'I was thinking of... *The Ghost Writer.*'

www.ingramcontent.com/pod-product-compliance
Lightning Source LLC
Chambersburg PA
CBHW050951050726

47592CB00007B/2529